Loving Again

BOOK 2
in the
Second
Chances
SERIES

PEGGY BIRD

author of *Beginning Again*

CRIMSON
ROMANCE
F+W Media, Inc.

Published by
Crimson Romance
an imprint of F+W Media, Inc.
10151 Carver Road, Suite 200
Blue Ash, Ohio 45242

www.crimsonromance.com

ISBN 10: 1-4405-5192-8
ISBN 13: 978-1-4405-5192-5
eISBN 10: 1-4405-5189-8
eISBN 13: 978-1-4405-5189-5

This is a work of fiction. Names, characters, corporations, institutions, organizations, events, or locales in this novel are either the product of the author's imagination or, if real, used fictitiously. The resemblance of any character to actual persons (living or dead) is entirely coincidental.

Dedication

For Maggie, Max, Sophie and Ben.
I love you, but this is as far as you can read.

Chapter One

"Finally. The last load out the door." Amanda St. Claire plopped herself on a footstool with a sigh. Most of the friends who'd been helping her pack for her move had just left, taking a truckload of boxes to her storage unit. Only Sam Richardson remained, a man who got her more hot and bothered than all the packing and moving in the world could. However, after what had happened last year, it was hard to know how to handle an attraction that was clearly mutual but which so far, other than one kiss—one wild, passionate kiss—she'd managed to keep tamped down.

She cleared her throat, which was closing in just thinking about that kiss. Or maybe it was the dust she'd inhaled while she was packing up the basement. Sure. Dust. Like that made her breathless. It would probably be better if he left, too, and let her figure this all out when she was in Seattle and he was here, in Portland. "Sam, you don't have to hang around. You got suckered into helping when the only reason you were here was to say good-bye."

"Funny, I don't feel like a sucker," he said. He was standing way too close. She swore she could almost feel his breath when he spoke, his voice low and husky, creating goose bumps all over her. And those eyes—warm, chocolate brown with an unreadable expression—amused, maybe affectionate. Maybe she shouldn't overthink this and just enjoy the way he made her feel.

God, he was sexy. She'd wondered for months if there could be something between them. But her life had been so messed up by what happened last year that she wasn't sure she could rationally say she was in any position to find out. "Sorry, that sounded unappreciative and you know I'm not. I'm just feeling guilty. I owe you more than I can ever repay and getting you involved in packing boxes of books for two hours wasn't how I envisioned trying to make it up to you."

"I keep telling you, you don't owe me anything, Amanda." He shrugged those broad shoulders of his, then grinned. "On the other hand, I'm not above playing on your guilt if it gets me dinner with you tonight."

She ran her hands through her curls that hadn't seen a comb or brush since early morning. "Dinner? I don't know. It's tempting but after the day I've had I'm not sure I'm up to going anywhere."

"I was thinking more like getting a pizza delivered." He pulled out his cell phone. "I have the best pizza place in Portland on speed dial."

She paused before answering, knowing it probably wasn't smart to start anything the evening before she was leaving for six months, before she had a chance to sort out how she felt about . . . well, pretty much everything. But instead of the "no, thanks" her head was telling her to say, her heart—or maybe her hormones—got control of her voice and squeaked out, "Pizza would work." After she took a deep breath to get her voice under control, she said, "But first, I need to get out of these clothes and take a shower. Digging around in the basement I've avoided like the plague for years got me filthy and sweaty."

The expression he had on his face now wasn't hard to read at all. "I'll volunteer to help with that, too, if you'd like," he said, his voice rich with innuendo, as he tucked one of her wayward curls back behind her ear.

"Thanks, cowboy, I think I can manage it all by myself." Although the feel of his fingers on her face and the idea of having him help her shower certainly made her heart beat a little faster.

When he smiled this time she noticed for the first time that he only had one dimple. How'd she miss that? It was cute. He was cute. Also hot, good at packing boxes and a genius at saving a girl's life.

"It was worth a shot," he said. "Okay then, if I can't help, tell me what you like on your pizza."

"My favorite is a Margherita."

"Thought that was a cocktail," he said.

"Mozzarella, basil and tomato." She caught yet another of his amused expressions. "But you knew that, didn't you?" Before disappearing up the steps she added, "And help yourself to a beer. I think there's still a six-pack left in the refrigerator."

*

Sam wasn't sure what he'd expected when he stopped by her house. Not sure exactly what he wanted to happen. At least that's what he told himself. His excuse for going to her house was to say good-bye, to give her a small gift, to see if it would be okay if he visited her in Seattle. But if he forced himself to think about it for more than two seconds, he would have to admit he wanted more. He just didn't know how much more she was willing to give him the night before she left.

The first time he'd seen her it was like he'd been hit by lightening. Stuck his finger in a socket. Been Tasered. Something that jolting. But he'd kept his distance. At the beginning, it was because she was with someone else, even if she said he was not exactly a serious boyfriend. Later it was because things got complicated. Assuming that's what you call having the woman you want arrested for murdering her son-of-a-bitch, cheating, low-life, not-exactly-serious-boyfriend.

And Sam was part of the organization that had done the arresting. No matter how much he helped her, he was still a police detective and she had been seriously unimpressed by the officers of the Portland Police Bureau. For the arrest, for ignoring what she'd found proving her boyfriend Tom Webster had been involved in drug dealing with a couple of dirty cops; for refusing to look further to find Webster's real killer; for almost killing her by failing to send her to the hospital after she was badly beaten. Hell, for all he knew, she hated the bureau and everyone in it for merely existing.

He'd never believed that she'd killed Webster. Not once in the times he'd talked with her, including the night of the murder, had there been any indication she was capable of that. And if that hadn't convinced him, what he'd seen a couple weeks after Webster's death would have. She'd been beaten and terrified in her home by hooded bad guys looking for something they said Webster owed them. No one could have been as convincing in her innocence as she was without actually being innocent. Not in his experience. She was a gifted artist, not a talented actress.

She was innocent and in danger that night. He'd risked his career by taking her from the scene to get medical attention when the responding officers hadn't moved fast enough. He'd been put on administrative leave for interfering with procedure. But it was worth it. She'd had a pneumothorax—a collapsed lung—and much more delay could have been fatal. The up side was being on leave meant he'd had the time to help her defense attorney.

He succeeded. He found the evidence that identified the real killer, another of Webster's girlfriends who'd set up Amanda as the perp. After the charges had been dismissed, the police took a second look at the case. Following up on information Amanda had found, they arrested a handful of minor dealers and thugs and the cops who'd siphoned drugs off from their busts to sell through Webster's club, maybe even at the restaurant he ran in a building Amanda owned. Some of the bad guys were already in prison. The rest were awaiting trial.

Now, instead of being part of an organization that had her under arrest, he was her savior, a role he didn't like any better. The one he was interested in was quite a bit more intimate.

In the three years since his divorce, joint custody of two sons and a job that sucked up huge amounts of time had made any sort of social life difficult. Then he met Amanda and knew he'd do whatever it took to overcome those obstacles if she was interested.

In the time he'd spent with her during her trial, he'd realized it wasn't just attraction he felt for her, it was also admiration. She was simply the most amazing woman he'd ever met. He'd seen her physical bravery when she was beaten, seen the steel in her spine when she was in court. He'd also seen her talent—he'd first met her at an exhibit of her glass art.

And she packed a whole hell of a lot of beautiful into a small package. She was barely five feet tall but those wild, caramel-colored curls, that full, sensual mouth and gold-flecked hazel eyes, that curvaceous body . . .

An image of that body naked in the shower upstairs flashed through his mind. He shook his head to get rid of it. Damn. What that woman did to him. He hadn't been on the dating scene for years but he was pretty sure it was still tacky to present a woman you've promised dinner to with a hard-on and no food.

He headed to the kitchen, his cell phone in hand, to cool off with the beer she mentioned. Then he had a pizza to order.

*

A half hour later, clad in clean T-shirt and jeans, Amanda was at her breakfast bar attacking the pizza. Sam had set the table using a roll of paper towels as both plates and napkins and opened two beers.

"I must have been more hungry than I thought. Or else this is the best pizza I've ever had. Thank you. Once again, you've saved the day." She picked up her third piece and wolfed it down.

He drained his bottle of beer and took the last bite of his first slice. "You enjoy food. I like that about you. Although I have no idea where it goes. You're not exactly well-padded."

"And what would you know about the state of my padding, Detective Richardson?"

"I'm a cop. I'm good at making visual assessments, Ms. St. Claire."

"Well, since in your expert opinion I don't look too padded, I think I'll have another piece."

When the pizza was gone, Amanda added the paper towels and pizza box to a large black garbage bag under the sink. As she straightened up from the task, she rolled her shoulders.

"I can't believe I'm this sore. Not even the shower helped. You'd think with all the heavy stuff I lug around in my studio, I'd be able to manage a few boxes of books."

"No matter how heavy those sheets of glass of yours are, you don't have to move them around for eight or nine hours a day. And it was more than a few boxes of books today from what I saw." He came up behind her at the sink. "Here, let me see if I can massage out some of the kinks." He began to knead the muscles in her shoulders and, using the pads of his thumbs, to do the same to her neck.

"Ah-h-h. Perfect. This is exactly what I needed." She rotated her head and stretched her neck. "God, that feels good. If you ever need a second career, you could do this for a living. I'd write a recommendation for you." Her body moved with the force of his massaging, her hair brushing his chest, then her back arching toward him. She could feel the heat of his body, felt her heartbeat kick up a notch at the pleasure of having his hands on her.

He continued down her back, massaging one vertebra at a time. Somewhere in the middle of her back, however, she could feel it become more caress than massage, could feel his breathing join hers in ratcheting up. She slumped back to close the space between them, resting against his chest, hoping he'd take the hint. He did, beginning to nuzzle her neck. "M-m-m. That feels wonderful, too, Sam."

"Amanda." His voice was thick and husky. "I . . ."

She turned to see a questioning look in his eyes, as if trying to assess what her reaction was to the change of direction. To answer she reached toward him, put her hand at the back of his neck and, as she drew him toward her, felt him embrace her. She'd thought about being in his arms for months and now she was.

Bending his head, he lowered his mouth toward hers. She lifted her face and was about to close her eyes when she felt him hesitate.

"Is something wrong, Sam?"

"Nothing's wrong. Just . . . are you sure about this?"

Standing on tiptoe, she answered him, pressing first her lips then her body against his. His mouth opened under hers and all of his hesitation disappeared.

It was no gentle kiss. She could feel every ounce of his hunger and desire, passion and longing. His hard body pinned her against the cabinet. His fingers threaded through her hair, tipping her head to the angle he wanted so he could kiss her even more fiercely. Then his tongue found hers and she gasped at the pleasure of it, the velvet feel of tongues sliding and slipping over each other in what they both knew was the rhythm of what was to come.

Skin. She needed to touch his skin. She pulled his shirttail out from his jeans and slid her hands up under it to his back, to the muscles she could feel flex and move as he repositioned her so his thigh was tucked between her legs, the thick erection she could feel behind the zipper of his jeans pressing against her belly.

Warm, wet arousal pooled between her legs as he rocked his hips into her, pushing harder against her. She moaned into his mouth as he found his way under her T-shirt to her breasts. This massage was so sensual she wanted it to go on forever.

He broke from the kiss but didn't let up on the pressure of his body against hers. "I've wanted you since the first time I saw you, thought about this but . . . "

"But our timing sucked."

"It still does. You're leaving."

"We have tonight. We don't have to waste it."

"And you're sure?" He asked again as he pulled back and looked in her eyes.

She was sure of one thing. She'd decided while she was in the shower, he wasn't leaving her house tonight until she got him into her bed. The events of the year before had ruined so much. She wasn't going to let them ruin any more.

"Yes. But if you're not sure yet, I'll just go upstairs and wait for you. When you make up your mind, it's the second door on the right. I'll leave a light on for you." She turned to go but he reached for her hand. He was laughing.

"We better go together. I might get lost."

She led him to her bedroom, strewn with more boxes and her suitcases but she didn't think that would matter to him. She was right. He didn't seem to pay attention to anything but her. Coming up behind her, he carefully slid the T-shirt over her head.

"This is like unwrapping the best present at Christmas." He cupped her breasts in his hands and kissed her shoulder. "I love it that you don't wear a bra. I don't have to fumble around because I can't figure out how to unhook the damn thing."

She giggled a little, suddenly nervous, but he turned her around and kissed her with deep, seriously long, hot kisses, stealing her breath, reminding her why she wanted this. When she put her head back, gulping in oxygen, he moved down to her neck, kissing the pulse in her throat, nipping at the notch between her collarbones. All the oxygen in the universe couldn't keep her from feeling dizzy with desire.

In spite of his claims that he fumbled with women's clothing, he had no trouble with the zipper on her jeans or with easing them over her hips. She kicked off her sandals and shimmied the jeans the rest of the way off until they fell to the floor. Clad now in nothing but a scrap of lace, she was aware of how naked she was. From the flare of desire in his eyes she knew he was aware, too.

He led her to the bed, she lay down and he sat beside her. He dipped his head to one breast, teasing the nipple with his tongue, while he massaged the other breast, rolling the hardened nipple between his thumb and forefinger. She arched toward him, as if to bring her breasts closer to his mouth, as a hunger for him increased with each touch, every kiss.

Wanting to feel his bare chest against her, she tugged at the buttons on his shirt, her fingers shaking with desire, finally getting them undone. He worked the cuffs and she slid the shirt down over his shoulders until it joined her T-shirt and jeans on the floor. She wrapped him in her arms, drew him to her, felt her sensitive nipples brush against his hard chest and sighed with pleasure.

But he backed away. She made a soft sound, objecting to the loss of his heat, her arms reaching for him, until she saw he was only shedding his boots, jeans, and boxer briefs. Before he came back to her, he pulled his wallet out of his jeans and removed a foil packet, placing the condom on her bedside table.

If the thought occurred to ask him why he was carrying condoms around, it was smothered in a kiss. And in the thrill of having him run hands down her body until his fingers found the top of her lace thong. When he'd helped her wriggle out of the last barrier of clothing between them, she pulled him close to her, their arms and legs twined around each other. She rocked her hips against his and walked her fingers down his stomach to his thighs, touching the velvety tip of his erection, but he caught her hand, raised it to his lips and kissed her fingertips.

"Let's take this slow, baby. We're in no hurry."

As if to prove his point, he didn't touch her anyplace but her face, tracing around her mouth, her nose and eyes with his forefinger, then kissing each place in turn. "You're so beautiful.

Even in jeans and a T-shirt with dust streaks on your face you were beautiful."

"You don't have to say that, I'm already in bed with you."

He gave her a mock serious look. "There are a few rules with me. The first is when I tell you you're beautiful, you say, 'thank you, Sam' and you don't give me attitude."

"Thank you, Sam." She suppressed a laugh. "Any more rules?"

"Later." He went back to exploring her with his fingertips and mouth, back again to her throat, her collarbones and her breasts. "Right now, I'm busy."

This time she couldn't keep the laugh under wraps. "So, you like rules, do you?"

"Hell, yes. I'm all about rules. Why do you think I'm a cop? Rules, regulations, laws. I'm in my element."

"And do you always make your women laugh in bed?"

"Yeah. Sometimes, even on purpose."

She was still smiling when he turned the conversation serious again by making love to her mouth, slowly and sweetly at first then fiercely, demanding she join him in the passionate play of lips. As their tongues explored and played feint and parry, their hands roamed over bodies hot with desire, discovering the texture of skin, finding the places where pleasure lay, warmed by the heat they were generating.

When he finessed her legs apart and slid one of his legs between hers, she urged him on with her hips, wanting him, ready for him, needing him.

But he only skimmed the palm of his hand over her again creating a tingle that spread down her belly. His hand seemed instinctively to follow the path to the place between her legs where the feeling pooled.

He stroked her with his thumb; his fingers slid inside her, moving in a slow and sensual rhythm until the tingle became a burn, then an intense fire. Just when she thought she couldn't bear it any longer, he withdrew his hand and she moaned, wanting it back. He seemed to ignore her little sounds of protest as he moved down her body until he was between her legs. His hands on her hips, he began an agonizingly slow progress of kissing her from her knees to her thighs.

When he reached her sex, just the feel of his breath on her was almost enough to make her come. With his fingers he gently parted the folds protecting her clitoris and kissed her there. She moaned again, this time with pleasure as he licked and sucked, circling her most sensitive place with his tongue and nipping gently with his teeth until he took her over the top.

As the waves of climax subsided, he moved back up along her body until he could kiss her again. She tasted her own arousal on his lips as he ravaged her mouth. Aching for him, her body craving his, she shifted restlessly against him. When he finally handed her the foil packet so she could cover him, she wanted him inside her so much she had a difficult time opening the condom and fumbled putting it on him, her hands shaking.

He took it from her and, guiding her hand, helped her unroll it over him. Then taking his time, he entered her.

"Christ, you feel good," he said into the ear he was kissing.

"You have no idea how good I feel," she said, "I didn't know I could feel this good." She rolled her hips against him, groaning with pleasure as she finally felt him fill her. He felt so hard, so hot, so amazing.

"Don't move," he whispered, his voice thick with desire. "Stay still."

"But . . . "

"Not yet. Let me just feel how good it is." His hips didn't move as he nibbled at her mouth, first her top lip, then the bottom. He explored inside her mouth, caught her tongue with his teeth, gently sucked on it.

She caught fire again. "Oh, God, Sam, please . . . " She covered his face with kisses, urging him on.

But all he did was go back again and again to the pulse in her throat and to the hard tips of her nipples, tonguing them, raking his teeth across the sensitive skin.

Just when she thought the delightful torture would never end, he brought her legs up around him and slowly, deliberately, began to rock their bodies together, gradually increasing the tempo, moving to another climax. With their bodies joined, their breathing synchronized, they climbed together until first Amanda, then Sam took the roller coaster down the slope to the other side.

They held each other afterwards, trying to make the journey back to being two separate people. After his breathing had returned to normal, Sam tilted her face up so she was looking at him.

"Any way Seattle can wait?"

"Even if I was willing to turn down a residency at the best glass school in the country, I need time away from Portland, from everything that happened last year. Besides, I've shipped most of my studio to Seattle so I can work after my stay at Pilchuck and I have a house sitter who . . . "

"Stay with me then until you can unwind everything. Go to Pilchuck later. We've been dancing around this . . . " he indicated their entwined naked bodies, "for months now. Stay and let's see where it takes us."

"This is like my conversation with my parents. They want me back in Shaker Heights so they can help me see where the next phase of my life takes me, to quote my dad."

He ran his fingertips down her flank. "This isn't more convincing than a telephone conversation with your parents?"

Laughing, she took his hand and kissed it. "Yes, Sam, it is. You're considerably more tempting, I admit. But it doesn't change the answer. Whatever the next step is, I have to make the decision, not someone else, no matter how well meaning. Besides, you deserve a woman who . . . well, who's not me right now. I don't know how I feel about anything."

"Suppose I told you that doesn't matter."

"It does to me. I could hurt you and I'm not going to hurt the person I owe my life to."

"You don't . . . " He stopped. She assumed he saw the stubborn set of her face because when he spoke again, he tried another tack. "Okay, how about we make a deal? You have your time in Seattle. I'll come visit you after you get out of your residency, just so you don't forget what I look like. Then, when it's over, you come back to Portland so we can see if we can work it out between us."

"I haven't decided about coming back to Portland yet." The disappointed look on his face made her hurry to get to the next sentence. "But absolutely come see me after Pilchuck. And I promise I'll talk it over with you before I decide what's next after the six months. That okay?"

"No, I like my deal better. But I'll take yours if that's all I can get."

Tracing the lines around his eyes and mouth with her finger, she said, "You're the most incredible man I've ever met. And I'm probably the biggest idiot on the planet for walking away from you." She put her arms around him and held him, nestling into his chest. "But I have to get my life back together, prove I can take care of myself. And going away is the only way I can get it done." She rolled over and looked at the clock. "And it all starts very early tomorrow morning when the movers arrive to pick up what goes to Seattle."

"Is that a hint for me to leave? Thought it was the man who wanted to be alone after sex."

"Is it? I don't know. I've never had a one-night stand before."

He pulled himself up on one elbow and took her chin with the opposite hand. "I don't know what tonight is. It could be the beginning of something or the end. But it's no one-night stand. Not for me. And I don't think for you either."

"You have a lot of experience with one-night stands, cowboy?"

"Enough to recognize that this wasn't one."

"Okay. I'll take your word for it. We'll figure out what it is—was—later." She kissed him lightly on the lips and slid out from under the sheet. "For now, how about I get dressed and walk you downstairs. We can say good-bye there."

When they got to the front door, he held her and made her promise she'd be in touch as soon as she got to Seattle. After he released her from his embrace, she picked up a large, cardboard box from the table in the entryway and handed it to him.

"I was going to have this delivered to you. Not that it's close to paying you back for what you've done for me—I'll never be able to do that—but I want you to have it."

He opened the box. Inside was a bubble-wrapped package with a metal stand taped to it. "Is this what I think it is?"

"If you think it's a piece of my work, it is. It's the first piece you ever saw, the night we met."

"I don't know what to say. Except thank you." He looked inside the box. "Does it have the title anyplace on it? I don't remember what you called it."

"It's called 'Hope', the piece is called 'Hope'. Which is exactly what you gave me at the worst time in my life."

*

She didn't find the small box he'd left on her kitchen counter until the next morning. In it was a glass charm on a fine gold chain. On the charm was a delicate brush painting of bamboo. The note with it said: *"Amanda—This is from the Chinese Garden. You said once it's your favorite place in the city. I'm told the bamboo represents strength, resilience, and grace—exactly what I've seen in you over the past months. I hope you'll wear it occasionally and think of a beautiful place in Portland. And me. Sam."*

Chapter Two

Four and a half months later

Goddamn traffic. How did people put up with it every day? Sam hadn't been able to leave Portland until three in the afternoon, which meant he ended up right in the middle of Seattle's famous rush hour traffic. At the rate he was going, he'd miss the whole opening. Which, given what the past few months had been like, shouldn't have surprised him.

Amanda's last night in Portland had been better than anything he could have hoped for but the time since had been a goat fuck. For three months, they talked, emailed and texted while she was tucked away at the Pilchuck Glass School. Then, when she moved in with her best friend from college so she could continue her work, they began to talk about getting together in Seattle.

For six weeks, they tried to make it happen. But three of the weekends were out because of his every-other-weekend with his sons. On the weekend they'd finally nailed down plans, he pulled a seventy-two-hour shift on a messy double murder. Then she was out of town celebrating her friend's birthday. Nothing had worked. So, when she mentioned the opening at the Erickson Gallery for an exhibit of the work of Pilchuck students that included her, he decided he'd take a couple vacation days and just show up without telling her he would be there. What could screw that up?

Apparently, the traffic, which had him at a dead stop, looking at Boeing Field, not at her or her work.

*

Amanda couldn't decide which was more uncomfortable, feeling hot and sweaty or nervous and twitchy. On one hand, she was miserable from the very un-Seattle-like ninety-degree heat. On the other, her anxiety level about being on public display for the first time since her trial was too high to measure. The only thing pushing edgy-anticipation-of-catastrophe out of gold medal contention was, when it happened, at least it would be over. The TV weatherman said the heat would hang on for a few days.

For what seemed like half an hour, Amanda had been trying to get through the crowd to the back of the room where Cynthia Blaine, her best friend and current roommate, along with Cynthia's boyfriend, Josh, were waiting with cool water and soothing words for her. But people kept stopping her to congratulate her on her work.

She envied Cynthia and the other artists with work in the exhibit. They were enjoying the evening. Of course, all they had to do was sip wine, make arty small talk and flirt. Amanda had to enthusiastically discuss her new work while staying on high alert for some unknown calamity.

Finally she made her way to the back of the gallery. Kicking off her platform sandals, she took the paper napkin her friend offered her, blotted her forehead and sighed. "I'm hot."

"You certainly are," Cynthia said. She handed a glass of ice water to Amanda. "By the number of pieces you've sold tonight, you're about the hottest glass artist in Seattle and that, my friend, is saying something."

"I was talking about the weather, but thanks." She wiggled her toes on the cool tile floor and gulped down the water. Glancing around at the crowd she said, "It feels like something weird's going on, doesn't it? I mean, nothing terrible has happened so far but . . . "

Cynthia rolled her eyes. "Everything's going great. Try to relax and enjoy this, will you? God knows you've earned it." She reached into her purse and, with a "ta-da" flourish, brought out Amanda's favorite Dagoba chocolate bar. "Here, see if this helps."

Amanda swapped the now-empty glass for the candy. "You're wonderful. I was too nervous to eat before I came here and my stomach's paying me back by growling."

As she nibbled on the sweet she continued to inspect the crowd. Surely there were people here who remembered what had happened in Portland. Who would resurrect the scandal first? That woman over there who looked kinda reporter-ish? The man who kept staring at her? Would it happen here, tonight, or would she have to wait for the newspaper tomorrow? What if . . . ?

Dear God, she had to stop this. Not only was she driving herself crazy, but she was sure her friend found her way past "annoying" on the Richter Scale of Irritating Emotions. Starting soon after the five o'clock opening, Amanda had forced Cynthia to accompany her around a conversational loop that quickly rutted from wear as she begged to hear over and over that the evening was going okay.

Now, more than two hours later, somewhere in the middle of the eighth, or maybe tenth, circuit of the reassurance loop, Cynthia's attention wandered, mid-sentence, apparently caught by something she saw over Amanda's shoulder.

Amanda felt the blood leave her face. "What's wrong? What did you see?" Cynthia only smiled, still looking into the distance. Amanda tensed, what remained of the chocolate melting on the fingers she clutched around it. "Tell me. Please!"

"Calm down. It's nothing bad," Cynthia said. "This sexy guy just sauntered in, out of a Levis' ad if the jeans and cowboy boots are any indication, and he's staring in this direction. When I smiled at him he didn't respond. So, unless he's all *Brokeback Mountain* over Josh, that leaves him looking at you. Do you know him?"

Jeans and cowboy boots? Amanda swallowed hard, trying to shift gears from panic to a feeling she didn't recognize at first. A flicker of optimism? A little shiver of anticipation? She shook it off. It couldn't be. He wouldn't. Besides her gut told her nothing good was in store for her tonight, only something bad.

And she was tired of waiting for it. She wanted the ax to drop, the sword of Damocles to fall, the roof to cave in. Pick a cliché, make it happen, and be done with it. Then she could say, "I told you so" and go back to Cynthia's apartment where—please, God—it would be cooler.

But, no, she wasn't headed out of the gallery. She was staring at her friend who was grinning about some random guy in Levis. She knew Cynthia would pester her until she looked, so Amanda turned around, her eyes down. If this was the messenger of doom she'd been expecting all evening, it was time to get it over with.

When she looked up, however, her breath stopped for a heartbeat or two. It was no stranger or harbinger of disaster. It was Sam; all 5'11" of him, broad shouldered and slim hipped, in a white shirt open at the neck and boot-cut jeans with his ubiquitous cowboy boots. He was standing near the front door, people streaming past him like water around a rock, looking directly at her.

He'd starred in so many of her fantasies while she was in Seattle, she would have sworn she remembered every detail about him. But seeing him now she realized she'd forgotten just how flat-out sexy he was even standing still, his feet shoulder width apart, his hips tipped forward, his shoulders squared, his thumbs hooked into the front pockets of his jeans.

And how could she have forgotten that she could feel the warmth of his eyes across a crowded room?

His mouth she remembered, pressed against hers, turning her insides to liquid. The sun-streaks in his sandy-brown hair and the tan forearms showing under the rolled up sleeves of his shirt, she remembered, too. They reminded her of the horseback rides they'd talked about but never taken.

Cynthia was right. He was sexy and delicious—and staring, waiting for her to acknowledge she'd seen him. He nodded hello when she did. When his smile became a grin, a flutter of something light and free flew from the middle of her chest, released the breath in her lungs and untied the knots in her shoulders.

"Oh, my God, Sam . . . " The candy bar slipped from her fingers, leaving Cynthia to lunge for it as Amanda deserted her for the front of the gallery.

When she got to him, all Amanda could say was, "It's really you." When he touched the glass charm she wore around her neck, she clasped his hand to her chest where she was sure he could feel her rapidly beating heart.

"I hear a rising young star in the art glass world is here tonight. Know anything about that?" he asked.

"There are several. You looking for anyone in particular?" She couldn't seem to stop smiling, or let go of his hand.

With his left hand he tucked a curl behind her ear as he studied her face. "You look . . . well."

"I'm doing okay. Except for being nervous about the exhibit. Wondering if it's a mistake to present myself in public so soon after . . . well, you know . . . that kind of thing. I'm glad to see you, though. I was going to call this weekend, try again to get together now that this show is . . . " The sentence was left dangling as she tried to calm her pulse, now at aerobic exercise levels, with deep, slow breaths. But that only brought in the smell of his clean, woodsy aftershave, which didn't help calm anything. "Are you in Seattle for a meeting or something?"

He freed his hand and pulled a handkerchief from his pocket. After he wiped a smear of chocolate off his fingers, he removed a smudge of it from her mouth. "No, like I said, I heard there was a hot new artist exhibiting here tonight."

"You drove all the way from Portland for this?"

"Yeah. Don't I at least get a hug for that?"

She slipped her arms around his waist and nestled against him with a sigh. He held her close and rested his cheek on the top of her head. It felt so good to be in his arms again.

Without her heels on, she didn't quite reach his shoulder so when he released her from the embrace, she stood on tiptoe and turned her face up to get him to bend and kiss her. He didn't need much encouragement to give her a light butterfly of a kiss that awakened a dozen of its butterfly friends in her stomach.

"I'm so glad to see you. It has been so long," she said.

"Four months, two weeks and six days, if anyone's counting." The dimple in his right cheek deepened and his brown eyes lit up as he smiled again.

"Apparently you are. Does that mean you missed me, cowboy?"

Ignoring her question, he draped an arm across her shoulders. "Since I must win the prize for driving the farthest for your opening, doesn't that get me a personal tour of the work I fought through hellish traffic to see?"

"If you'll stop complaining about the traffic like Portlanders always do, I'll introduce you to some people and then show you around."

When they got to the back of the gallery, Amanda said, "This is Cynthia Blaine, Sam. I worked in her studio in Seattle. Cynthia, I'd like you to meet . . . "

"Oh-my-god-Sam, I believe you said as you dropped half of your favorite chocolate bar," Cynthia said. "Hi, nice to meet you."

"And this is Josh Franzen." The two men shook hands.

"Sam is . . . Sam Richardson . . . is a friend I haven't seen in a while," Amanda said.

"Right. He's the guy you . . . " Cynthia began but changed direction when Amanda shot her a fierce look, afraid her friend would reveal exactly how much she talked about him. " . . . the guy who helped your attorney," Cynthia finished and glared back.

"I'm going to give Sam a tour of the show," Amanda said as she picked up her sandals. "You mind? We won't be long."

"Don't worry about us. We were about to leave for Bellingham anyway," Cynthia said.

"I forgot about that. Say hello to your parents for me," Amanda said. Holding on to Sam's arm for balance, she reshod herself, then kissed her friend good-bye.

As she led Sam through the show, she pointed out her work, three sets of two pieces on the theme "Contrasts."

"Interesting," he said. He was examining a pair titled "War" and "Peace," pebbles of glass on curves holding up a clear glass center shot through with strands of wire. "It's more abstract than the 'Emotions' series I saw last year. I like what you've done with the metal and the glass."

"I spent part of my time at Pilchuck experimenting to see how to get it to go together the way I wanted it to. And I'm still working on it." She described creating the three-dimensional objects of glass, metal foils and slender wire. As she did, she proudly pointed out the red dots, indicating pieces already sold, which had broken out like measles on the tags identifying the pieces.

"I had to be talked into being part of this show, but I have to admit it's the best one I've ever had, not that I've had that many shows. I've sold all of the pieces already, to serious collectors and at higher prices than I've ever gotten. I wasn't sure what the response would be, but the previews were good and so far this evening everything seems to be going okay. It's such a relief . . . " She stopped. "I'm babbling, aren't I? Sorry. I've been nervous all evening."

"Nothing to apologize for. You should be excited. But looking at these prices, I'm glad I already own an Amanda St. Claire piece. I don't think I could afford you now."

"I could always work something out for you, Sam."

"How about working out time for dinner with me tonight, then? Or do you have plans?"

"Max, the gallery owner, said a collector wanted to talk to me after the reception but she left so I'm not sure it's still on. Let me *check.* Look around for a minute and I'll find out."

When the gallery owner said that the collector had left satisfied with her purchase and the earlier conversation, Amanda arranged to meet Sam at the bar in the hotel where he had a reservation for the night.

At eight-thirty, he was waiting for her with a glass of her favorite wine and a space next to him in an intimate booth. He had the same grin on his face he'd had in the gallery.

They clinked glasses and sipped. "I still can't believe you're really here," she said. "That you drove all the way here for the opening. But I'm awfully glad to see you. We have so much to catch up on. I don't even know where to start."

"Why don't we start by figuring out a place to eat? Any ideas about where you'd like to go?"

"About that," she said as she pulled an iPhone out of her small purse.

His expression went from warm affection to cool distance and he sat back in the booth, watching her. "It's okay. If you can't do dinner, we can just talk until we finish the wine. At least I'll have had a chance to see you . . . "

"Stop over-analyzing, Detective Richardson. I'm not looking at the time because I'm planning to ditch you, I'm figuring out how long it's been since I let the beast out."

"What beast?"

"Chihuly."

"Dale Chihuly, the famous glass artist?" He sounded confused.

"No, Chihuly my curly coated retriever puppy. He and all his litter mates were named for people with curly black hair."

The affectionate smile was back. "And how is it having a puppy to take care of?"

"A challenge. Among other things, he chews on anything he can get his mouth around when he's been left alone too long. Which is why I'm looking at the time." She slipped the phone back into her purse. "Why don't you come home with me while I take care of him and then we can eat in the neighborhood?"

*

Chihuly and Sam were introduced. The dog was walked, watered and fed. Her shoes now safe from her pet's mouth for another couple hours, Amanda led Sam to the Italian restaurant a block away. After they'd ordered, she said, "You haven't asked the obvious question yet about whether I'm coming back to Portland. How come?"

"Thought I'd enjoy the evening before I hear the answer I think I already know." He took a sip of wine. "I don't know that I've ever seen you look this happy. And I can hear the excitement when you talk about your work. It must have been a great residency."

"Beyond my wildest dreams. You saw some of the work tonight. It'll take years to exhaust what I learned there."

"So, let's put off the bad news 'til I kiss you good night."

"What makes you think that's gonna happen, Sam?"

He picked up his wine glass and took another swallow, avoiding her eyes. "I guess I'm not surprised. Your emails lately could have been sent by my sister and we haven't talked in a week or so." He swirled the wine in his glass for a few moments, then sat up and turned to face her. "On second thought, might as well get it over with. I assume you won't be coming back to Portland. That right? "

She smiled at him. Tore a piece from the baguette in the breadbasket, dipped it in the dish of olive oil and had a bite.

"Are you enjoying watching me twist in the wind, Amanda?"

"I have to confess, I am. I've never seen you off balance before. And I doubt I will any time soon again so let me have my moment." But she couldn't hold out against the anguished look in his eyes. "Okay, like I said, I've had a great time here, professionally. Personally, I wanted to be back in Portland. I missed the city."

She shook her head. "No, that's not entirely accurate. I missed Portland, all right. But mostly I decided I wanted to see if the deal you offered me was still good." It was her turn to drop her eyes.

After a deep breath, she looked up again. "I was going to call you this weekend, I really was, to tell you I was coming back to Portland. Assuming it matters to you. Next month. I mean, that's when I'm moving." Her eyes searched his face, trying to find the answer she wanted to see there.

Before Sam could say anything, the waiter brought their entrées, then came back with a pitcher to freshen their water glasses.

After the server left the second time, Amanda said, "So? No reaction? I thought you might like what I just said."

He carefully cut a piece of his chicken cacciatore, chewed it and swallowed it before he answered. "Wasn't sure how you'd react to my showing up in Seattle unannounced. You were happy to see me but you glowed when you talked about your time here. I thought about that after I left the gallery. Wondered if you'd be telling me you're staying here."

"So—you're saying, what? You psyched yourself up for me to stay here? Is that what you want?"

"God, no."

"Then, have you changed your mind about the deal?"

"The deal?"

"The one where I came back to Portland so we could see if we could make it work out between us. If I move back will you . . . can we . . . ?"

"Amanda," he interrupted, "do you really think I drove all the way up here to see an art exhibit? I mean, I love your work but I came to see you. I had to find out what was going on. It's been driving me nuts."

"Then what is all this reluctance about—payback for not being in contact for a while or for saying I liked seeing you off balance?"

"I'm not reluctant. I don't understand what you meant when

you said I couldn't kiss you good night."

"No, I meant that you were expecting bad news but there wouldn't be any."

"Didn't sound like that. It was either no kiss or . . . " He snapped his fingers and said with an innocent expression, "Oh, wait. You meant you didn't plan to say good night to me tonight."

"You think I invite men to sleep over on our first date?"

"First date? We're way beyond first date, aren't we?"

"Have we ever had dinner out before tonight?" He shook his head. "Gone to a movie?" Head shake again. "Had anything that even vaguely resembles a date?" He opened his mouth to answer and she quickly said, "Rides to the ER don't count." He smiled and shrugged his shoulders.

"I mean, think about it. Yes, we've known each other for over a year and we've slept together. But it hasn't exactly been a normal boy-meets-girl, has it? I know how you act in an emergency and how well you do your job but I don't know what the M stands for in your name or whether you like to dance or swim."

She waved her fork around as she continued with the list. "I don't know whether you're a morning or a night person. Where you went to college. Whether you went to college. I don't even know how old you are, much less when your birthday is. Somehow we never got around to that kind of thing, what with a murder trial and drug dealers battering down my door."

He laughed. "I guess I agree. Well, except for the sleeping together part. I don't recall any sleeping that night." He ignored her eye roll. "I admit we've done things in reverse but didn't you say you'd make an exception for me."

"That was about a piece of art, Sam, not relationships or sex or what-ever-it-is we're talking about now."

"So, what *would* you like to do for the rest of the evening?"

"How about we finish our dinner and then go home and have dessert. We can talk about it." Before he could answer, she said,

"There's ice cream in the freezer and my roommate is gone for the weekend."

"You've convinced me. And, since you asked: October 9th and I'm thirty-six. The M is for Martin, my mother's family name. I swim okay but I grew up on a ranch so I'm better on horseback than in the water. I have a business degree from the University of Oregon and I'll let you find out on your own about the morning/night thing. Maybe even soon."

"What?"

"You said you didn't know those things about me. Now you do. Except for the last one."

"Oh." When what he meant about "the last one" finally sunk in, she smiled. "*Oh!*"

"Your turn."

She laughed. "What is this, the Cliff Notes approach to dating?" When he nodded she continued. "Okay, well—February 14th and I'm twenty-seven."

"Oh, hell. I thought you just looked young. You really are young, aren't you?"

"You make it sound like I'm jail bait."

He started to say something but she stopped him. "Do you want to hear the rest or not?" He nodded. "My middle name is for my godmother and I hate it although I love her. But if I tell you, I expect that you will never, and I mean never, use it." She waited until he acknowledged the ground rule. "Okay, it's Minerva."

It was obvious he was trying hard not to laugh. "That'll be an easy promise to keep. I can't think of any circumstances under which I'd call you Minerva."

"Good. And for the rest—I love to dance. I'm a pretty good swimmer but I grew up with horses so I'd rather ride, too. I have an arts degree from Reed College. I'm more a morning person although I do all right at night if I have a good reason to be up."

He raised an eyebrow at the last response.

"Oh, please. I meant that if I get involved in something I enjoy, I can be a night person."

"That's what I meant, too."

"I'll ignore that. And you forgot one."

"I did?"

"Yeah, do you like to dance?"

"Only the really slow ones." He motioned to the waiter who brought over the check.

"Well, we can work on that," she said as she slid out of the booth.

*

While Sam walked Chihuly one last time, Amanda got out ice cream, chocolate syrup, whipped cream and maraschino cherries and made sundaes for them. When they were finished eating, Amanda took the bowls back to the kitchen. She returned to the living room to find Sam had put music on.

"Is that Chopin?" she asked.

"Yeah, the nocturnes." He listened to a few bars. "The second."

"Not what I'd have thought you'd pick. I would have imagined you'd have settled for my Jimmy Buffett."

"Which stereotype we working from here: cowboy or cop?"

"Busted. Sorry."

"My mother was a classical pianist. I grew up with Chopin, Rachmaninoff, Mozart, Glass, Gershwin. You name it, if it was piano music, we had a recording of it. Or she played it. And speaking of stereotypes—you and Jimmy Buffett? I'd have thought you were more the Norah Jones type."

"One of the guys plays Jimmy in the studio and I've gotten to like him."

"You have all sorts of interesting quirks, don't you?"

She glanced up at him and looked around for a napkin. "And

you have all sorts of chocolate syrup on your mouth." She reached to wipe his mouth. "Here, let me . . . "

"Let's try the way I wanted to get the chocolate off your mouth in the gallery," he said and gathered her into his arms.

His mouth was soft and cool; he tasted of vanilla ice cream, chocolate syrup and the all-male flavor she remembered as "Sam." He kissed her tenderly, like a sweet and gentle first kiss. When her lips parted, he circled her mouth with the tip of his tongue so softly she almost thought she imagined it. He broke from the kiss. "Better?"

"Oh, yes," she said, having no idea whether there was still syrup on his mouth or not, and reached for him again.

This time he took possession of her lips with an ownership that left her breathless. His hands moved up her back and to the sides of her breasts while his tongue did magic tricks in her mouth. She matched his intensity with her own, months of longing flavoring their kiss and fueling the passion of their embrace.

When they came up for air, he traced the outline of her lips with his index finger as he said, "Any chance you can amend those first date rules of yours?"

"I'm thinking seriously about it."

"How about we find someplace more comfortable for you to think about it?"

She led him down the hall to her bedroom. When they got there she kicked off her sandals and started to undo the ties of her halter-top that wrapped around her waist.

He came up behind her, reached around and stopped her hands. "Here, let me." He undid the knot, unwound the ends and released the halter-top, slipping it over her head. He drew her back against his chest and caressed her breasts until she made soft noises of pleasure and her breathing quickened as he nuzzled her neck while he teased her nipples with his fingertips until they were hard.

"Oh, Sam, that's…ah-h-h," she breathed out in a ragged gasp.

He unzipped and eased her pants over her hips until they pooled on the floor then he lifted her out of them, picked her up and sat on the bed with her on his lap.

"Now you," he said and put her hands on the first button of his shirt. When she had finished, he gently put her on the bed, stood up, pulled his shirt out of his jeans, unbuttoned the cuffs and stripped it off, his eyes holding hers the whole time. His boots and socks went next. He pulled a condom out of his wallet, put it on the bedside table and shed his jeans and boxer briefs.

He joined her in bed but when he began to slip off the scrap of lace she wore as panties, she stopped him.

"Do you always carry a condom in your wallet?"

He smiled and brushed a curl back from her cheek. "Not since I was a teenager."

"So has that been there for twenty years or did you bring it from Portland today?"

"Neither." The smile moved up to grin.

"Neither? Then, what? Come on, Sam. You're busted now. Give it up."

"The expression on your face today, in the gallery, when you first saw me. It was how I've always wanted you to look when you saw me. When you hugged me and looked up for me to kiss you, I thought, I wanted to think . . . anyway, when I walked past a drugstore on the way back to my hotel . . . "

"You figured you should be prepared in case you got lucky tonight."

He looked more serious now as he gently kissed her. "No, not like that. Not with you. I wanted to think that maybe you were telling me that the night in Portland was the beginning, not the end."

"Oh, God, I hope so," she said as she pulled him to her for a kiss that was neither gentle nor soft. As the kiss deepened, his hands began to wander to breast, to waist, to hips and thighs. Then his mouth found her breast, his tongue circled her nipples, first one, then the other. His hands brought her skin alive, brought fire and light to every cell in her body.

Separating her legs with his, he moved his hand to her sex. As his fingers slid into her on a flood of arousal, he circled her clitoris with his thumb. Gasping out his name, rocking against his hand, she rode to the edge of climax then over.

She closed her eyes, coming down from the incredible high he'd given her. But he was not finished. He came back to her mouth and their lips touched, their tongues explored and danced. Somehow, sometime, she wasn't sure when or how, he'd sheathed himself and now was slowly entering her, easing his way into her core. But she didn't want slow and easy. She wanted all of him. Now.

She wrapped her legs around him and thrust her hips at him, calling out his name, rocking hard against him, meeting him thrust for thrust, bringing them both to orgasm.

Afterward, she clung to him, her head in his shoulder. When she finally looked up at him, he said, "You asked if I missed you. I can't remember a longer four months. And do I care if you come back to Portland? Only about as much as I care that I wake up in the morning. That answer your questions?"

Chapter Three

The following month

The first time Sam had seen Amanda's studio, he'd gone there on police business, to talk to her about Tom Webster's possible illegal activities. Nothing about the day had been what he expected.

Starting with her studio. Outside, the building looked like a World War II Quonset hut. Inside it was more industrial than artsy. Boiler room-level heat radiated from three furnaces, the "glory holes" where the two glass blowers who shared the studio with Amanda melted the glass they used. Opposite the furnaces was a bank of kilns used both by the glass blowers and Amanda. She used them to fuse and shape her kiln-formed glass. Her studio mates used them for a controlled cool-down of their blown-glass pieces.

Across the back of the building, where Amanda worked, were deep slots constructed of plywood where she stored her glass: table-top size sheets in a multitude of colors: ruby red and royal purple, citrus shades of lemon and orange, the greens of spring and Oz, and all the blues of the sea, the sky and Paul Newman's eyes. Above the sheet glass were clear jars full of various sizes of colored granules along with tubes of something looking like multi-hued spaghetti. Frit and stringer, Amanda called them.

And Amanda—the beautiful young artist he remembered from the gallery where he'd first met her had greeted him dressed like she was ready to do construction. Her curls had been pulled back from her face, held in place by some kind of clips. She'd worn no make-up and a heavy, long-sleeved T-shirt. Her jeans had been splattered with something pink and her shoes looked heavy enough to survive hiking the Himalayas.

Nothing had changed from a year ago. Amanda was even dressed the same today.

"How come you get stuck with all Amanda's packing and unpacking, Sam?" Leo Wilson, one of the glass blowers—and one of the friends who'd helped Amanda pack before her move to Seattle—asked as Sam made his way to the back of the building. "We have to do it. She's our landlord. You're a volunteer." The semi-smirk on his face was evidence that he knew exactly why Sam kept volunteering.

"Big fan of glass art. Glad to have another talented artist back in town."

"That explains this time . . . " Leo began.

Amanda cut him off. "Leo, unless you want a rent increase, you better leave the help alone." She reached up and kissed Sam on the cheek. "Thanks for doing this. I really appreciate it. I apologize for my mouthy studio mate."

Surprised—and pleased—that she'd been so possessive, Sam circled her waist with an arm. "No problem. I want to make sure you're good and settled so you don't run off again. I hear there are good glass schools in North Carolina and New York."

"Don't forget Rhode Island, Australia, England and Italy," she said with a raised eyebrow and a half-smile.

"Christ, I better get you moved back in ASAP so you're not tempted. What can I do?"

Two hours later, the boxes she'd had shipped back from Seattle were unpacked, the contents put into their correct places, as were the dozens of sheets of glass Amanda had purchased from Bullseye Glass the day before. She was just about to take Sam out for coffee when his pager went off.

"Sorry, baby," he said when he got off the phone. "I was supposed to have the afternoon off but . . . " He shrugged his shoulders. "Maybe dinner tonight? About seven? Your place?"

"You're on." She kissed him again, this time on the mouth.

"And thank you again. I don't know what I'd do without you."

"I don't intend to let you find out," he said.

Ten minutes later, Amanda got a phone call that pulled her, too, out of the studio.

*

"Just because she's gotten decent reviews for that show in Seattle and sold a few pieces of glass, she thinks she's some kind of star," Eubie Kane said. "She's not; she's a thief. And she's avoiding me because she's afraid I know."

A tall, slender man in his mid-twenties, Kane paced in front of the checkout counter at the Bullseye Resource Center, the retail store for the glass manufacturer. As he walked back and forth, his voice grew louder with each sentence, powered by wind milling arms and a rising tide of indignation. Clad in worn overalls and a dingy T-shirt, he looked more like a panhandler at a freeway exit than the artist he was. "But now that I know what she's been doing, she's going to have to . . . "

"Eubie," manager Felicia Hamilton interrupted, "keep your voice down. I called her. She was unpacking her studio and forgot she promised to meet you. Why didn't you just go over there in the first place?"

"I wanted to meet her here." Kane shifted his backpack as if it contained a great weight and continued pacing, much to the amusement of the other artists there to purchase glass for their projects and the students who'd been drawn in from the classroom space adjacent to the retail area by his loud voice.

"If I let her, she'd always have some damned excuse about being busy." Kane swung the backpack off his shoulder, sideswiping a pyramid of jars full of granulated glass, causing it to teeter, like a near miss in some carnival game. Ricocheting from that almost-disaster, he banged into the cart of a woman waiting to pay for her supplies, sending ten large sheets of glass tipping forward. A half-dozen people rushed to save the glass from crashing.

The manager motioned to Robin Jordan, the instructor whose class had become part of the audience, to get other customer carts piled with glass out of Kane's orbit. "She has been busy. She just moved back to town; she's got a show coming up in Tacoma, commissions from her Seattle show."

"Right. The great Amanda St. Claire, busy doing work based on *my* ideas. And you're covering for her, treating her with kid gloves because she's a good customer."

"Oh, come on, Eubie, we treat all our artists with kid gloves," Felicia said in a cajoling tone. "We treat you with kid gloves, don't we?"

"Yeah, sure." His scornful expression showed what he thought of that statement. "She gets special treatment, even uses your big kiln when no one else can."

"I don't think Amanda's ever asked but the answer for her would be the same as for anyone else. We only rent out the small kilns."

"That's bullshit. A guy who knows one of your staff told me she does."

"Give me your source and I'll get this straightened out. Amanda has never . . . "

"I've never what, Felicia?" Amanda asked, coming in the door.

"Used our big kilns," Felicia said. "Eubie says we let you use them."

"Nope, never. Except for class projects the time I was a guest teacher. When I need a kiln bigger than the ones in my studio, I rent Kent Simon's Skutt. Is that what you wanted? You should have told me. I can ask Kent to contact you."

"That's not it and you know it." Kane pulled a magazine out of his backpack, opened it to a dog-eared page and thrust it in her face. "Did you think I wouldn't see this?"

Amanda immediately recognized the piece about her work. "I hoped a lot of people would see that article."

His forefinger rat-a-tat-tapped a beat on the page. "That piece of glass on the top left is a direct rip-off of my work. You saw my layered blocks on weather moods in the Glass Art Society exhibit two years ago and you duplicated them with different names."

"That's from a series I did about five years ago, before the Glass Art Society exhibit."

"You're lying. That's my idea you stole." He spit the word at her. "People have been commenting on it. You've built your career on my back. So you'll have to compensate me or I'm going to sue you. I came here to warn you." Turning abruptly, he stomped out the front door.

The students who'd been watching the performance ebbed back toward the classroom, avoiding eye contact with Amanda. Customers carefully examined the coding labels on the sheets of glass as though they'd never seen them before.

Felicia finally broke the silence. "Well, that little meeting worked out nicely, don't you think?" she said with a wry smile, her blue eyes sparkling behind her Ben Franklin glasses.

"What bug crawled inside him?" Amanda asked.

"Not sure what it is but I'm pretty sure I know where it is," Felicia said. "Only thing I can't figure out is why. He can be whiny but he's usually not obnoxious. Have you heard about this before? I haven't."

"This is the first for me, too. I've met him once or twice. Saw his work at the Glass Art Society and at The Fairchild." Amanda shook her head. "He's on a tear for some reason. This is all I need." The sound of customers moving around caught her attention. She saw that people were still avoiding her and shook her head again. "Sorry, not your problem. Apologies all around. If you hear any more about this, call me please?"

Returning to her studio, Amanda tried to get back to work but she couldn't concentrate. She decided to run errands hoping retail therapy might help.

The shopping list for her studio wasn't long but, preoccupied with Eubie Kane's accusations, she couldn't focus, passing by the items she wanted in the office supply store two or three times before picking them up. She did notice a young man with longish dark hair who seemed to be in every aisle she was, making her uneasy. He reminded her of Eubie Kane and she didn't need to be reminded of him.

She blitzed New Seasons Market for studio snacks and something for dinner with Sam. Then she dropped in at the bank. In both places, she saw a man who looked a lot like the guy from the office supply store. Or else she was imagining Eubie Kane look-alikes behind every rock.

Back at the studio, she parked directly in front of the door. She was closing up the back of her SUV when a beat-up Toyota hatchback parked a few spaces behind her. She swore it was the same car she'd seen at the coffee shop where she'd stopped for a latte and it gave her the creeps.

Running through the big roll-up door that was, as usual, open to ventilate the heat from the glory holes, she called to her studio mates to go with her to check it out. But when they got there, the car was empty. They hung around waiting for the driver's return but after about five minutes, when no one showed, they went back into the building.

*

It was hidden behind old rhododendron bushes somewhere along the back of the house. Not exactly a precise set of directions but he'd figured it couldn't be too hard. However, what he found when he got in the backyard wasn't so simple. A confusion of greenery had grown together in a living wall that blocked access to the foundation.

When he tried to force his way behind the shrubs, thorns snagged his shirt, scratched his hands and face. Overgrown rose bushes were intermingled with broad- leafed shrubs covered in green buds. The shrubs must have been ten feet tall. To squeeze behind them he had to break off branches and tear at the leaves.

But there it was. Finally. The hardware was old, easy to jimmy. He got the door open and went into the basement. A phone rang upstairs and a dog barked. The security system was still working, it seemed.

Not long after he went out the side yard gate to his car, the blond from her studio pulled into the driveway, went into her house and was back out in less than ten minutes.

As soon as the car disappeared around the corner, the observer started his engine. If he did this a few more times, she'd have the motion sensor taken off that door and he could get in at his leisure. He congratulated himself that this phase of his plan, recovering the reward he was due, was coming along.

And so was the part about settling the score for what she'd done. He was sure he'd scared her following her around. He smiled. That was only the beginning.

Chapter Four

"I met with her," Eubie Kane said, "and I really made her sweat." He was having coffee at a café a couple blocks away from the scene of his confrontation with Amanda. With him was a man who could have been his brother—tall, dark-haired, young, although more muscular than the slender artist. "And you should have seen the reaction I got from everyone in Bullseye. That was inspired. I'm glad I took your advice."

"Dude. You're rocking it." His companion put up his hand for a fist bump.

"And I'm going to tell Liz Fairchild about my other opportunity, too, like you suggested."

"That only leaves Bullseye."

"I'm not sure I can get what I want from them. They're different."

"Maybe. Maybe not. I'm sure we can come up with a plan."

*

Amanda finally felt at home. After days of moving furniture back to the way she liked it and unpacking boxes, her books were in the built-in bookcases, her favorite leather couches were arranged around the stone fireplace, the Persian rug and low table were centered between them.

In the resettled dining room, she'd set the table for dinner. All she needed was Sam. He said he'd be there at seven but had called to say he'd be late. He offered to bring take-out. She'd turned him down, saying she wanted to cook a meal in her own home. She didn't add "cook a meal for you" but she thought he might have figured it out.

He arrived with a six-pack of beer and a bottle of her favorite pinot gris. As he rummaged around in a kitchen cabinet for a wineglass, he asked, "Did you get the rest of your studio settled?"

Amanda busied herself with the chicken breasts she was broiling, not sure how to answer him. She must have taken too long because when she straightened up from poking around in the oven, he was staring at her as if trying to figure out why she hadn't said anything. "Well, I guess you can say I'm settled, but . . . "

"What's the 'but,' baby? You look worried."

"God, Sam. All I seem to do is dump my problems on you. I hate it. Doesn't it bother you?"

"What's going on?" He had his cop face on now. Sadly, she knew it all too well.

After another long pause, she gave him the highlights of her confrontation with Eubie Kane that afternoon at Bullseye. She ended by saying, "I can't afford another scandal. Not after last year. My career would be buried forever. It makes me wonder if I should have stayed in Seattle after all." She was sure she had tears in her eyes and not from the heat of the oven. "Is threatening me like that against some law or another?"

"First of all, don't let this asshole send you running back to Seattle. Second, Kane's talking about a civil suit. That's not against the law. Unfortunately. Talk to an attorney. He—she—can help you. Do you know a good corporate-type attorney?"

"I guess I could call the man who helped me set up my business."

"Do it. First thing Monday." He handed her a glass of wine. "And don't let Kane spoil your homecoming."

"It's hard not to."

"Maybe I can help you out." He cocked his head and raised one eyebrow.

"What did you have in mind?" The frown lines between her eyes disappeared as she waited for him to say what she was sure he'd suggest.

Taking her into his arms he said, "How about I spend the night? I'm not scheduled for work tomorrow. We could sleep in. Or something."

"Hmm. Sleeping in. That sounds like fun."

"Maybe something more interesting might occur to us. Something even more fun than sleeping." He kissed her but before the kiss got too involved, he pulled away and stared at something over her shoulder. "But if you don't get those chicken breasts out of the oven, we're gonna have the fire department join us in our evening."

When she disentangled herself from his embrace she saw the smoke pouring out of the oven. "Oh, crap. Maybe we'll have to get take-out after all."

*

When he woke the next morning, Sam was alone in bed. Chihuly was curled up asleep on the rug next to Amanda's side, and he could hear the sound of the shower running in the bathroom. Unsure of what it meant that she had disappeared so quickly after waking, he debated whether to dress and go downstairs to start coffee or join her in the shower. The thought of her body wet from the shower, her beautiful breasts with those dusky pink nipples waiting to turn hard and pebbly from his mouth, made up his mind for him and brought him out of bed with an erection hard enough to split a brick.

He knocked on the door to the bathroom but she didn't answer. He could hear her but wasn't sure if she was singing or talking or what. It sure as hell didn't seem like the sounds of a happy woman after a night of hot lovemaking.

Taking a chance, he opened the door. He could feel the cool draft follow him in and knew she would feel it over the top of the shower enclosure, too. "You want some company?" he asked as he knocked on the enclosure door.

"Sure," she replied. "Come on in. Like they say, the water's fine."

He opened the door and stepped in as she turned her back to the shower spray to make room for him. He reached behind her, traded what he had in his hand for what was on the soap dish. When he pulled back he said, as lightly as he could, "You sound awfully sad—or serious—this morning."

She touched his face lightly. "I was just thinking how special you are, how lucky I am. But how sad it is that all I seem to do is ask you to solve my problems. "

Taking the washcloth she was holding, he soaped it up and then he began to rub the cloth over her breasts and abdomen. "There's a difference between depending on someone else to take care of you and sharing things that worry you with someone who cares about you."

"It doesn't feel like I'm just sharing. More like I'm depending."

"Am I complaining?"

"No, you're . . . oh, God, you're . . . "

He drew her against him and made long, lingering strokes down her back and butt with the washrag.

"You're changing the subject," she said.

"Is that bad?" The washcloth was on the floor and his arms were around her waist in less time than it took to draw a breath. The kiss he gave her wasn't a sweet "good morning" kiss. It was more an "I want you right now" kiss. When he broke from it, he asked, "How about changing the subject to this?" He retrieved the condom he'd put on the soap dish and handed it to her.

"How?"

"I'll show you. Cover me." She tore open the packet and rolled the condom over him. Light as she was, he didn't have any trouble lifting her so she could wrap her legs around his waist. As he pressed her against the wall of the shower, he went back to kissing her, doing to her mouth what he desperately wanted to do to her body—make love with fierce intensity. But he had to be sure she was comfortable with the idea. He drew back far enough to look deep into her eyes, trying to see.

"It's okay, baby," he said. "I've got you. You're safe."

"I know I am. Believe me, I know."

For the first time he could see in her eyes the beginning of what he wanted to see there—not just passion but trust.

Carefully, his back to the shower so he took the brunt of the spray, he slowly guided her onto the tip of his rock-hard penis, wanting to give her the time she needed to feel comfortable. But he didn't have to. She was there already.

She ground her hips against him, her nails bit into his shoulder, the passionate moans she was making echoing in the shower. That's what pushed him over the edge—the sounds. With one thrust he was inside her, driving himself in up to the hilt. In what seemed like only a few moments, they both found release.

When he could feel her breathing return to normal, he lowered her to the floor, still maintaining his hold on her until she was again in control of her rubbery muscles. Even then he didn't want to let go of her. He kept one arm around her as he rinsed them both off and turned off the water. He pulled a bath sheet off the towel rack and dried first her, then himself off.

They stepped out of the shower and he wrapped a fresh towel around his middle. As he watched her wrap herself up in the bath sheet, he said, "Whatever happens, I want you to know you can rely on me. Not to make it all go away but to be there when you need me."

"You've been there for me since the first time I saw you, Sam. I wish I could say I'd returned the favor."

*

"Amanda, I can't tell you how glad I am to see you looking so splendid," Mr. Todd said as he sat across from her at the dining room table in his floating home at a marina on the Columbia River. The sliding glass door, which framed snow-topped Mt. Hood in the distance, was open slightly to let in a breeze. The river was alive with sailboats and wave-runners jockeying for air and space.

As Sam had suggested, she'd called Mr. Todd's office the Monday after their dinner, to discover he'd retired from his law practice but his former secretary gave her his home phone number saying Mr. Todd would be happy to talk to her. With a bribe of dinner, she'd gotten an appointment with him that evening.

"And the food you brought was delicious." The white-haired, eighty-ish attorney had finished up a plate of grilled shrimp, sesame noodles, and tossed salad, and his blue eyes were wandering to the plate of brownies on the table in front of him. "I hope my legal advice is up to this standard."

"I was surprised when I was told you'd retired," Amanda said. "I thought you were going to be there until they carried you out on a gurney."

"When I realized I enjoyed sitting here watching the river as much as I enjoyed the view from the twenty-first floor, I knew it was time to leave a full-time law practice. But I made a list of a handful of clients I'd be willing to see at home. You were at the head of the list. So, tell me your problem."

Amanda summarized her run-in with Eubie Kane and ended by saying, "So, what should I do? Is this even an area of your expertise?"

"It's not one I'm familiar with, no. Art law is a specialized field particularly when it comes to issues like copyright."

"I've never filed a copyright for any of my work."

"Even if you haven't registered it, for both the visual and literary arts, the creator holds the copyright from the moment of creation.

47

There may be subtle differences between literary arts and fine arts and crafts, I don't know. But I can find out for you." He took two brownies from the plate, nibbled at one and started to speak again. "And I can also . . . " The doorbell interrupted.

A woman was at the door. "Hi, neighbor," she said. "I've got the olive ciabatta rolls you asked me to pick up for you. And I added an éclair because I know how much you like them." She handed him a bag, a small white box and a handful of change.

"Thank you for both, although my doctor wouldn't approve of the addition."

"I'll never tell, if you won't."

He glanced over his shoulder. "Do you have a minute? I'd like you to meet someone."

"I have nothing but time for you." The woman followed him to the dining room.

With a sweep of first one hand then the other, he introduced the two women. "Margo Keyes, meet Amanda St. Claire. She's a glass artist and a client of mine."

"For heaven's sake. I've always wanted to meet you, Amanda," Margo said, "I have a piece of your work—Serenity, it's called—from LOCAL 14 about four, maybe five, years ago. It's my favorite piece of art."

"Good," Mr. Todd said. "You're a fan. Amanda has a problem and you might be able to help me help her." He turned to Amanda. "Margo is not only my neighbor but she's a deputy district attorney."

Amanda had smiled at Margo's praise. Now the smile froze into an expression of distrust. "A DA?" Thanks to her recent experience with the criminal justice system, the DA's office was almost as high on her shit list as the Portland Police Bureau.

"Yeah," Margo said. "Me and the boys and girls in blue get the bad guys off the street."

"Not always . . . " Amanda began.

48

"Oh, God, how insensitive." Margo reddened with embarrassment. "I'm so sorry."

"Why don't we get to the reason Amanda's here," Mr. Todd said.

"While you do that," Margo said, "I'll work on getting my foot out of my mouth."

He gave his neighbor a thumbnail of Kane's threat and asked if she had any advice, other than finding an attorney who specialized in art law.

"Not sure I have any advice, but I can tell you there's been litigation around copyright involving glass artists that might give you comfort, Amanda. The first was a case about jellyfish and the other was Dale Chihuly suing over his designs."

"I remember the Chihuly case," Amanda said. "It settled out of court, I think, and the terms weren't made public. But I believe the guy Chihuly sued still had a career when it was over and that says something. What's the jellyfish one?"

"Guy sued another artist for doing glass representations of jellyfish like the ones he did. The case was decided for the defendant because natural forms aren't subject to copyright. More importantly for you, the court ruled the technique the second artist employed was in common use and wasn't subject to copyright either."

"Based on that precedent," Mr. Todd said, "if Amanda can show she's using commonly practiced techniques, there's not much to Mr. Kane's claim, is there?"

"Probably not, but if he's lawyered up, you need to be, too, Amanda," Margo said. "Can you give her a couple names, Mr. Todd?"

"I plan to. Anything else you'd recommend?" he asked.

"Dating your work earlier than the time he claims you saw his might help."

Amanda said, "Your piece is part of the series he accused me of basing on his ideas. Maybe the organizers of the LOCAL 14 show have records of what was exhibited that year."

"In my insurance file I have the receipt from the piece I own. There must be a date of sale on it," Margo said. "I'll make a copy and get it to you. And please take this seriously. Even if he's got no case, Kane can make your life difficult with bad publicity."

"Wonderful. Bad reviews and pickets for my next show. No gallery owner will want to represent me." Amanda closed her eyes for a few seconds, sighed and opened them.

"Thank you both for your help. This thing has made me very uncomfortable. I wish I knew what set him off." Amanda realized she had been chewing on her thumbnail and stopped.

"What set him off is less important than getting him shut down," Margo said.

"Yes, absolutely." Mr. Todd nodded his agreement. "But once you have a lawyer retained, you'll be prepared for whatever Mr. Kane's next move might be."

Chapter Five

Monday was the day Amanda worked on studio accounts and pulled phone duty. She didn't mind doing the bills but the phone calls, she swore, were never for her. She was wrong this week. The first call was from her alarm company. The sensor on her back basement door had gone off. Again. Just like it had for her house sitter while she was gone.

When she went home and inspected the basement, the door was still open. She couldn't tell whether someone had gotten in and gone through the boxes she'd not yet unpacked or whether it was a mess because she'd left it that way. She decided to take care of it later and returned to her studio.

Where she got two more calls.

The first was from Cynthia Blaine in Seattle, asking if she could stay with Amanda in a couple of weeks when she came to Portland to deliver some new work to The Fairchild Gallery. Amanda was happy to return her old friend's hospitality.

That was followed by a call from one of the tenants in a commercial building she owned.

"Amanda, Drake Vos. I'd like to talk to you about the lease for the restaurant. Are you available for lunch today?"

"Sure. What time?"

"How about right now? I'm parked outside your studio."

She walked from the office past the glory holes to find Drake Vos on the sidewalk outside the overhead door, leaning against the front fender of his black Lexus. At forty-eight he was almost old enough to be her father, but somehow she never thought of him that way. Maybe it had something to do with his tall, dark, and yummy good looks or perhaps the warmth in his eyes when he looked at her. He'd been hired by Tom Webster to run his restaurant in the building Amanda owned when Webster opened his club. After Webster's death, Drake had been a godsend keeping the restaurant running in the face of terrible publicity and had been doing a great job building the business back up.

She laughed at the "gotcha" look on his face, shut down the phone, and motioned him into the building.

Opening the trunk of his car, he extracted two large carry-bags. "If Mohammed won't come to the mountain . . . " He kissed her on the cheek. " . . . we bring the mountain to you."

"I know. I should have come in to see you but I've been slammed with work. Thanks for making the effort to come here."

She led him back to her part of the studio where he swung the larger of the two bags onto an empty worktable.

Waving him off, she indicated the office. "No, not that table. There'll be glass all over it. Go on into the office." She followed him and quickly cleared the top of the desk.

Vos pulled a tablecloth out of one bag, snapped it open, and let it settle onto the desktop. "I thought you'd enjoy what our chef's been experimenting with for now and the fall."

He pulled out two sets of flatware, dishes and wine glasses, a Thermos, and two square plastic containers. From the Thermos he poured a delicious smelling light-brown soup with wisps of foam on top. "Chef Jon calls this wild mushroom cappuccino," he explained as he handed a cup to her. "It'll be on the menu this fall when the mushrooms are available at a better price."

Amanda took a taste. "Oh, Drake, that's to die for."

Next he plated a spinach and sautéed scallop salad, which he explained was on the menu now. He added crisp rolls and placed the plates on the desk before positioning a folding chair across the desk from her. Last he brought out a bottle of pinot gris from the bag, removed the cork, and began to pour the wine.

"I don't drink at lunch," she protested as she put her hand over the top of her wine glass.

He pushed her fingers away with the neck of the bottle and poured a small amount for her. "Make an exception. This is a fabulous wine, nice body, tastes of apples and pears. You'll love it." He picked up his glass and toasted her. "Here's to our relationship."

"Mmm, it is good," she said after she sipped. She took a forkful of the salad. "So, you want to talk about the lease?"

"Lunch first, business second. We can talk about it after dessert."

"Dessert, too? I'll have to go home and take a nap."

He regaled her with bits of local restaurant gossip while they finished the salad and soup, after which he brought out a container of perfectly frosted, miniature chocolate cupcakes. "Cupcakes are becoming trite, I know, but I love them as a little bite of chocolate after a meal."

"Nothing made of chocolate will ever go out of style with me," she said as she took one from the container and ate it in two bites.

"I brought enough for you to share with your studio mates."

"If they're lucky." She picked up the last few crumbs of cake with her forefinger, which she licked clean. "Yum. Okay, now—business. What do you want to talk about?"

He poured the last of the wine into his glass and sat back in the chair. "The extension you gave me of Tom Webster's lease is about up and I was wondering what you plan to do about it."

"What I want is for us to reach an agreement so you can continue to run your restaurant. What do you need to make that happen?" She took a second cupcake from the container and nibbled at the edges.

"A good deal. I was wondering if we could extend the current lease for six months. After that, you can up the rent at regular intervals by whatever it takes to reach market rate over a three-year lease."

"That doesn't sound unreasonable. Let me review the old lease and talk to my accountant. I know things are tough for restaurants right now. I don't want to make it hard for you."

"Do you have the old lease here? We could look . . . "

"It's at home."

"Oh, you have a safe there, too?"

"No, why would you think I have a safe?"

"There are two safes at the restaurant. I figured anyone who'd have two in a commercial property she owned would have one at home."

"I knew there was one there. Tommy must have put the other one in."

One of Amanda's studio mates stuck his head in the door of the office. "Amanda, something weird is going on with one of the kilns; it's heating up too fast. Can you . . . ?" He stopped, his face registering the lunch scene. "Sorry. Didn't mean to interrupt."

"It's okay. We're finished." She got up and headed for the door. "I'll be back as soon as I see what's going on, Drake."

"It's okay. Take your time. I'll just clean up here."

When she returned from checking the kiln she found Drake looking through the cupboards along the wall behind the desk. "Can I help you find something?" she asked.

"Just looking for a plate to put the rest of these cupcakes on."

"There's nothing up there but office supplies. What you want is here." From a cabinet along the opposite wall she pulled out a plate and handed it to him. "Thank you, from all of us but especially from me. That was the best lunch I've had in ages. I'll call my accountant this afternoon and get back to you about your lease as soon as I talk to him. If he says it's a reasonable approach, which I imagine he will, I'll have my lawyer draw up the papers."

"I appreciate the positive response. Not that I expected anything else from the best landlord in Portland. Please come in for dinner soon. If you give me some advance notice, I'll even join you, if you wouldn't mind."

"You don't have to go to all that trouble, Drake."

"It's no trouble. You're not only the best landlord but the most beautiful one. It would be my pleasure." He kissed her on the cheek again, this time lingering a bit longer.

*

In spite of the wine and gourmet lunch, Amanda's afternoon was productive. That is, until she got one last phone call. It was from Margo Keyes.

"Amanda, have you hired a lawyer yet?" she asked.

"I have but I don't think he's heard anything back from Kane's attorney."

"Well, you might want to tell him Kane's been trolling the DA's office trying to get one of us to bite on his claim there's intellectual property theft going on under our noses. He says we're not doing anything about it because the thief is a prominent artist who's being protected. It doesn't take a mental giant to figure out who he's referring to."

"Oh, dear God. The point of hiring an attorney was to keep this under control. It's not working. What am I going to do? My reputation can't take too many hits like this. This will ruin me."

"Kane's reputation is the one at risk here. Call your lawyer. He'll tell Kane's lawyer to get his client under control."

"I'm not so sure Mr. Kane has anything to lose here. But I'll call my attorney. Thanks, Margo. I appreciate the heads up."

"And don't worry about this. Let the lawyers work it out."

Yeah, let the lawyers work it out, Amanda thought as she punched in the number for her attorney. But if they can't, I'm going to solve my problem myself. Whatever that takes.

*

Like most art venues, The Fairchild Gallery was closed Mondays. But on this particular Monday, Liz Fairchild was at the gallery hanging a new show. She could have tried to hide but it was hard to conceal an almost six-foot tall body topped by a mane of dark brown, henna-highlighted hair. Particularly when the body, dressed in an oversize white shirt and black leggings, was atop a ladder in front of a floor-to-ceiling display window. Eubie Kane found her by merely looking in from the street.

Liz wasn't particularly happy to see him. She sold his work in her gallery but he was a pain-in-the-ass to deal with. He was probably there to complain about something—again—or maybe to confirm the rumor she'd heard about him approaching another gallery to represent him. Whatever his reason for being there, Liz knew him well enough to know it would take him forever to get to the point.

As she feared, once Kane was admitted to the gallery, he wandered around, stretching his long legs and arms like a runner after a jog, rambling on about art, artists and galleries and the need for artists to be free to take advantage of the few opportunities offered them.

Liz listened for a while and then lost patience. "Look, Eubie, I have a show to hang. Let's cut to the chase. What is it you want?"

"Okay, okay. I want you to release me from my contract."

"So, you're giving me the required two months notice?"

"No, I want out now."

"Why would you think I'd release you now when you have your first solo show with me next month? A show I've already paid large amounts of money to advertise in a half-dozen publications." Discussions like this made Liz wish she hadn't given up smoking ten years before. Nicotine would have rendered Eubie a lot more tolerable.

"But I have a better opportunity, a chance to be in a real gallery, to be part of their annual emerging artists' show that all the critics review. But they won't sign me because I have a contract with you."

Liz wasn't sure whether she was more annoyed by his whining or his insults. "Honey, offending the person you want the favor from isn't a particularly effective way to get what you want." She ran her fingers through her hair. "So, the rumor's true. You went to The Woods Gallery and asked for representation."

"I'm willing to give up the solo show, if you'll release me."

"Either you're not listening or there's an audio problem in here that I never noticed before. So maybe if I write it, you'll get it." Liz took a marker, grabbed a scrap of paper from the floor and wrote in big, black letters, *Not only no but hell no.* She handed the paper to him saying, "You signed the contract. You live by it."

He snatched the paper from her hand, ripped it in two, and crammed it into the pocket of his overalls. "You'll be sorry you crossed me, Liz. I'm about to make my mark on the art world in Portland and you're gonna regret you didn't play ball." Kane attempted to storm out the door but discovered he had to wait for Liz to unlock it, taking most of the drama out of his exit.

Not five minutes after the young artist left, Mike Benson knocked on the door. This interruption Liz was happy to see. Mike was her temporary help while her regular staffer was off on an extended holiday.

"I thought I'd see if you needed anything for the new show." He stopped. "Hey, what happened? You don't look so happy."

"I'm not. One of my artists was here trying to worm his way out of his contract. He pissed me off." She shook her head. "But I'm glad you dropped by." She picked up a shipping box from the floor. "Will you finish uncrating these paintings while I make a couple of quick phone calls to see what I can do to get this thing with my artist settled?"

"Sure. I'll uncrate, you hang, and maybe you can get out of here at a decent hour."

"And I can buy you a late lunch."

"Thanks, but I've got plans later today. Hot date." He grinned.

In the back storage area, where what she laughingly called her office was located, Liz made her phone calls. When she returned to the gallery, the paintings were all uncrated and unwrapped, but Mike was gone, without telling her he was leaving, without asking if there was anything else to be done and leaving the front door, with her keys still in the inside lock, open. Young men, of whom she was inordinately fond under social circumstances, could be amazingly annoying under other circumstances, Liz thought. She mentally shrugged her shoulders and got to work hanging.

By the time she drove home a couple hours later, it was pretty clear that her day had sucked. First, there was Eubie Kane. Next, the painter from Arizona whose work she was hanging had sent different paintings than the pieces he'd promised, not all of which worked with the theme she'd planned for the show. Last, there was a gold bracelet missing from her jewelry display case. She wasn't sure who made her angrier: Kane, her featured artist or her new hire, who had to be the thief because she'd seen the bracelet in the case when she'd gone to make her phone calls but it wasn't there when she came out. As soon as she found the item missing, she'd called Mike. When she got voice mail, she remembered he'd said he had a hot date. She left a message saying she needed to talk to him urgently.

Halfway home she thought about dropping by his house and leaving another message but realized she didn't have his address with her and she didn't have the energy to go back to her gallery to get it. She drove to her home in southwest Portland, put on a mix tape of her favorite golden oldies, poured a large Bombay Sapphire gin on the rocks, and stewed about her day. She wasn't sure Mike would show up for work again but if he did, she was going to raise hell with him.

Chapter Six

Sam and Amanda had quickly fallen into a regular pattern of seeing each other. When he was with his sons for the weekend, Sam picked her up at her studio during the week for dinner and they had take-out Sunday evening at his apartment after the boys went back to their mom. The weekends when he was kid-less, they spent as much time together as his job allowed. They went to the symphony. They rode horseback. They took Chihuly to the dog park and played Frisbee with him.

Amanda loved being with him. He was constant in his attention and affection. He made her laugh. She found herself thinking of him often during the days she wasn't with him. Her heart beat faster when she saw him. All the signs of falling for him.

But she wasn't sure she was ready to get more involved. Not until she was standing securely on her own two feet. As a result of this reluctance, she changed the subject every time the conversation got within two states of any comment that could lead to a discussion of where the relationship was going.

It had been her bad judgment in getting involved with Tom Webster that had gotten her in trouble, trouble she couldn't get out of without a lot of help. She was determined never to let that happen again. Not that Sam was another Tom Webster. She knew that wasn't true. But she had to prove to herself that she could manage her life without help, even if that help came in the form of the sexy cowboy-turned-cop she was half in love with. So, she tried to keep their conversation light. Distracted him when it looked like it was getting too deep. Whistled for her dog who adored Sam to come play with them. Whatever worked to change the subject.

It worked. Until the beef bourguignon evening.

Amanda had spent the afternoon making the dish using Julia Childs's recipe. It had been a long time since she cooked anything that complicated and she'd forgotten how much work it was. But when all the ingredients had blended together, it was sublime, rich and beefy with just the right amount of garlic and herbs. Well worth the effort.

"What smells so great?" Sam asked when he arrived with a bottle of wine and a kiss for her and an ear scratch for Chihuly.

"Boeuf a la bourguignon."

He circled her waist with an arm. "I saw that movie. So, Julia's helping you cook this evening, is she?"

Looking up at him with a smile, she said, "Not a movie I'd have thought you'd pick."

"I didn't," he admitted.

"Ah-ha. A woman chose it for you."

"Yeah, my sister dragged me to it when she couldn't get her husband to go."

"I didn't know you had an older sister."

"How do you know she's an *older* sister?"

"I have a younger brother. I understand how us older sibs work." She held up the bottle. "Shall I pour this for both of us or would you prefer something else?"

"Wine's good. But let me."

He went in the direction of a corkscrew and glasses; she disappeared into the kitchen where she added crackers and grapes to a plate of softened Brie.

The wine was poured and her CD of the Grieg piano concerto was playing when she returned. Sam was ensconced in his favorite place on the leather couch. Joining him, she spread cheese on several crackers and handed one to him, then settled back, nestling next to him.

"Dinner's ready any time we are but it'll hold for a while," she said.

"Let's wait a few minutes. I haven't seen you all week." He touched his glass to hers. "I've missed you. Maybe we should . . . "

She handed him another cracker and interrupted. "Did you see Pink Martini's playing with the symphony in a couple weeks? I tried to get tickets but they're sold out."

He let the interruption go although his expression was more frustrated than usual when she changed the subject to something less intimate. "I have tickets for the Saturday night performance. I was going to ask if you'd like to go."

"How'd you do that?"

"I bought them when I renewed my symphony season tickets."

"Season tickets? I thought you just had those two we used a couple weeks ago."

"Nope. Whole season—well, part of the whole season. But you don't need to know the intricacies of the Oregon Symphony's ticket options. All that matters is . . . "

"I get to hear Pink Martini! I love you!"

"So, that's what it takes. I wondered."

Thanks to her outburst, the conversation was back to where she wasn't comfortable. To top it off, she couldn't tell how serious he was.

But he let her off the hook. "I can't sit here any longer smelling that wonderful smell. How about I help you get dinner on the table." Picking up their glasses and the bottle of wine, he headed for the dining room.

She'd dodged the bullet. For the moment.

When the Brie and wine, beef bourguignon, salad and chocolate mousse were finished, they stayed at the table drinking coffee, exchanging horse stories. Hers were about competing in dressage and jumping at her private high school in Ohio, his about his Appaloosa, Chief, and his rodeo experiences in Eastern Oregon when he was young. She bragged about her ribbons and medals on her horse Tiger Lil. He allowed that he'd won a belt buckle or two.

Then the conversation veered again.

"I've been meaning to ask—are you still getting false alarms from your security system?" he asked.

This was one of the subjects she'd tried to keep Sam away from. Even in her most paranoid moments, when she was afraid that the repeated alarms from the security sensor on her basement door meant the intruders from the year before had returned, she hadn't given in to the temptation to tell him about it. She was not going to be one of those women who ran to a man the first time she heard a strange noise.

But she wasn't going to lie to him either.

"I've had a couple more. I'm beginning to wonder if the sensor is faulty and maybe I should have it removed."

He was quiet for a moment, seeming to think about what she was saying. "There's nothing in your basement worth stealing, is there? If these aren't false alarms, if someone is trying to break in, they're trying to get in the house, aren't they?"

"I guess so. I never thought about it. What could anyone want in the basement? I don't keep anything valuable there. It's all dust and old clothes and boxes of stuff I can't quite part with."

There was another pause before he spoke again. "No one else has ever put anything there that you know of?"

"Who would . . . do you mean Tommy?"

"The men who broke in last year, they said Webster had something that belonged to them. They must have thought something was here."

"I told you then—Tommy never left anything in my house except the occasional disposable razor."

He flinched and she realized she probably shouldn't remind him that Tom Webster had slept with her in this house, too.

"You told me he had a key to your house. He could have gotten in when you were in your studio, couldn't he?"

"Yes, but . . . "

"Would you mind if I took a look around down there?"

"Didn't your colleagues do that last year?"

"It can't hurt for me to do it again. If I don't find anything suspicious, maybe it might be a good idea to have the sensor taken off the back door and put on the door from the basement to the kitchen."

She reluctantly agreed. "Okay. But I don't want to muck around down there. I hate being in the basement. It creeped me out before all this happened and last year only made it worse. I'll sit on the steps while you look around."

While she sat and sipped coffee, he looked through the small rooms that were the remnants of half-completed remodeling projects left by former owners. He poked at the ceiling in a few places and had just started knocking on a few walls when she said, "This is silly. There's nothing here. And Chihuly's scratching at the door behind me. He wants to be let out and I don't want to waste any more time here. I'm going to attend to my dog and start doing the dishes."

Sam looked like he wasn't convinced but he went back upstairs with her. As they cleared the table he brought up the other subject she'd been trying not to discuss.

"The other thing you haven't talked about is Eubie Kane. What's happening on that front?"

"Nothing." She avoided his eyes, picked up their wine glasses and headed for the kitchen.

He persisted. "Nothing? No response from him or his attorney?"

"That's right. Nothing." She had her back to him so didn't know how close he was until she felt his hand on her shoulder.

"Nothing? Or nothing you want to talk about?" He turned her around and lifted her chin with his finger so she had to look at him.

"I'm taking care of this, Sam. I don't need to be saved."

"I'm not trying to save you. I care about you, about what's

bothering you. And I have some experience in this area, you know. I might be able to . . . "

"Help. Yeah, of all people in the world, I know that, Sam. You bailed me out once. Big time. I can't let you keep doing that. I have to stand on my own."

"Amanda . . . "

"No more. We had this discussion before and nothing's changed since then. I need to take care of myself. Without being rescued like some stupid damsel in distress in a tower someplace."

He folded her in his arms and held her. "No one would ever mistake you for Rapunzel, baby. Just don't lock me out. Talk to me. At least let me be a sympathetic ear. Promise?"

"If you'll promise not to try to solve my problems."

"If that's what you want, sure." Then he kissed her softly and sweetly, a gentle, almost imperceptible touch of his lips on hers. When he outlined her lips with his forefinger, a yearning washed over her. In spite of her brave words, she loved his strength, felt safe with him. She had to fight the urge to dump it all in his lap so she could run away, lose herself in her work, maybe.

Instead, she tried to lose herself in his attention to her mouth as his warm breath feathered across her lips. Her breath stopped, the world stopped, while she waited for him to kiss her, really kiss her, as she knew he could. Finally, blessedly, he did. He tasted of chocolate and coffee and kissed like an angel. It was heaven to kiss him.

He drew her closer, one hand at the small of her back, the other at the nape of her neck, his fingers tangled in her hair. Angling his head, he took her mouth with his. This time it was no angel who kissed her but a man who showed her how much he wanted her with his mouth, with his tongue, with his body as he turned her insides to liquid fire.

His lips never moved from hers even when he adjusted his head to have better contact so he could steal the breath from her lungs with a gentle suction. Desire flamed over her as his tongue explored her mouth. At the same time his hands moved from the small of her back up her sides straying to her breasts, his thumbs grazing the hardening tips of her nipples.

She drew her head back, trying to catch her breath but that only gave him access to her throat. He kissed down the side of her face to the rapidly beating pulse in her neck and sucked gently at it. She could feel heat swirl around her belly and moisture pool between her legs.

"Let's take this to bed," he whispered.

She didn't answer, just moved to the stairs.

*

For a couple days, Sam chewed on the conversations they'd had about the basement and Eubie Kane. He didn't know what to do about the push-back he was getting from her when he asked about either subject, didn't know how to make her see that he wasn't trying to run her life, just be part of it. Hell, more than that. He was falling in love with her. He wanted her safe, happy. Wanted to help her make that happen.

But he'd been relegated to spectator, at least in the parts where she had any problems. He didn't like being useless. So to shake off that feeling, he did a couple things. He ran a background check on Eubie Kane, just to see what he could find out, which was nothing, not even a traffic ticket.

Then he asked around about the attorney Kane had hired. He was legit and high-priced, which led Sam to wonder where Kane was getting his money.

He also called the alarm company and found out exactly how many times there had been a false alarm at Amanda's. It was considerably more than he was comfortable with. He asked them to call him directly if it happened again after they notified her but without telling her. And he got a patrol car to swing by in the evenings just for good measure.

She'd be pissed as hell if she knew what he'd done. He'd have to take that chance. Because he couldn't just stand by and watch, even if she wanted him to.

*

"How come you're not with the sexy cowboy this weekend?" Cynthia asked as she hugged her old college roommate.

"He's got his two sons with him," Amanda said. "How come you're not with Josh?"

"He's at some political thing in Olympia." She extracted herself from the hug. "So we have a chance to talk about them both! Have you met his sons yet?"

"No, I don't know if I'm ready for that."

"How come? You're clearly in love . . . "

"Can we do this later? I'd rather see the new work you're bringing for Liz's gallery."

So, they talked glass and art for a while, then delivered Cynthia's jewelry to The Fairchild Gallery. Finally, back at Amanda's house, they cracked open a bottle of wine and began cooking dinner.

"Is this later?" Cynthia asked.

"Meaning . . . ?"

"You said we could talk about you and Sam later. Is this later?"

"I don't know, Cyn. It's complicated."

"As best I can figure out, that pretty much describes every male/female relationship on the planet. Why did you think yours would be different? Is he . . . ?"

"It's not him. It's me. I'm just not sure I can pull off a successful relationship."

"For heaven's sake, why? I mean, your last one was a disaster, but you had good relationships before."

"Really? Jim Warden?"

"Okay, not him."

"Bill McClain?"

"Or him." Before Amanda could add to the list, she said, "I get your point. But those were college guys. You're way past college now."

"And last year I got involved with a guy I was doing business with who turned out to be a cheating, crooked scum-bag. That's even worse than I did in college."

"Surely you don't put Sam in the same category?"

"Dear God, no. He's the most amazing man I've ever met. He's sweet and kind; he's smart and funny; he's . . . "

"Sexy as hell and great in bed."

"Sexy as . . . wait, how do you know what he's like in bed?"

"Because your face just told me. So, you're in love with him. What's wrong with that?"

"Nothing's *wrong* with it. It's just . . . I don't know. I'm just not ready for it."

"Not ready or scared?"

"Both, maybe. Not ready to admit what I'm feeling because I don't want to make another mistake. Scared I'm feeling this way to avoid taking care of myself."

"You've taken care of yourself since you were in college."

"Yeah, me and a huge trust fund I did nothing to deserve."

"Okay, you've had stable finances. But moving half-way across the country from your family, following your dream, establishing yourself as an artist . . . isn't that taking care of yourself?"

"I seem to be able to manage it in my professional life. I just suck at it personally. But," she pulled a pan of cornbread out of the oven, "I'm going slowly with Sam. Until I figure it out."

Cynthia ladled chili into bowls. "You've figured it out. You just haven't been brave enough to admit to yourself—and to Sam—that you're in love with him. That's all."

*

In the following weeks, Amanda's life seemed as golden as the remaining autumn leaves on the trees in her backyard. She heard nothing from Eubie Kane, who appeared to have crawled back into the weeds. The lawyers continued to negotiate, burning money she was happy to spend from the trust fund she knew could keep her in attorneys for decades. She wasn't sure that Eubie was in the same position.

Her professional life was blooming. The details of her solo show in Tacoma had been nailed down. A gallery owner from San Francisco contacted her about placing her work with him there. With her work in Liz's gallery as well as the Erickson Gallery in Seattle, she was in the happy position of worrying whether she could produce enough to meet the demand.

And her personal life? It was off the charts. Dinners, movies, and nights with Sam made the weeks rush by in glorious bliss. Cynthia was right. Soon she'd have to admit she was in love—first to herself and then to Sam.

*

After dinner one Saturday night, Sam said, "Are you ready to talk about something personal about us?"

"How personal?" She was sure she sounded wary.

"Meeting my sons. They're getting pretty curious about you."

She was sure she looked startled. "How do they even know about me?"

"They always ask what I'm up to on the weekends I don't see them. They've noticed that I'm going out more and Sammy, the older one, asked what the name of the woman was who was going with me. He prides himself on being a good detective."

"Like his dad." She closed her eyes for a moment. "I'm not sure.

How've you handled this before when you've dated someone?"

"They've never met anyone I've gone out with. After the divorce, their mother and I agreed we'd be careful about introducing them to people who would float into their lives and then walk out when the relationship ended. We didn't want to add any more stress than they were already under from the split."

"You get along better with your ex than some people do with their spouses."

"I don't know about that but we do have the same ideas on how to parent our sons. We agreed, no overnight guests when the boys are around and, like I said, no introductions to anyone unless it's more than a casual relationship. And this isn't a casual relationship any more. At least, not for me. But you have to decide if you're up for it. I haven't said anything to them but if you're okay with it, I thought maybe next Saturday you could have lunch or something with us."

She took a deep breath and made the leap. "Okay, I guess it's time. How about meeting at the dog park? If they hate me on sight, at least Chihuly will interest them enough to get us through an hour. But if everyone gets along, you could all come here for lunch."

"They won't hate you on sight but the dog park's a great idea. Jack wants a dog so bad he can taste it but their stepdad has serious allergies and I won't have one shut up all the time because of my hours. He'll love Chihuly."

The following Saturday Amanda sat on a bench in Normandale Park, her dog at her side. She wasn't sure who was antsier: her about meeting the boys or Chihuly because he was being made to stay while all the animals around him were chasing balls and Frisbees. But Amanda wanted him with her until Sam and his sons arrived.

She didn't get her way. At about the time Sam said they'd be there, Chihuly's ears perked up and, slipping out of Amanda's control, he took off running. When he ignored her calls to stop, she gave a long, sharp, shrill whistle and he came to an abrupt halt at the feet of two boys and a man who looked at Amanda in amazement.

"Christ, who knew you could do that?" Sam said as he circled her shoulders with an arm and kissed her.

"Sorry. Chihuly must have heard your voice. I didn't. That's the emergency signal that always makes him stop."

"Him and everyone else in the park." Sam gestured to the two boys. "Amanda, this is Sammy and this is Jack. Boys, this is Amanda St. Claire. And you've already met Chihuly." Sammy put his hand out to shake hers and looked at her with his father's brown eyes and serious expression. Jack had knelt to get to Chihuly's level and barely acknowledged the introduction until Sam asked him to stand up and be polite.

After his "hello," Jack said, "He has a funny name. What kind of dog is he? He's wooly, kinda like a sheep."

"He is, isn't he?" Amanda said. "He's a curly coated retriever. And he's named for a glass artist who has curly black hair."

"Does he do tricks?"

"He sits and stays although not today, I guess. And he fetches and rolls over. Mostly he likes to play Frisbee."

"Can we play Frisbee with him, Dad?" Jack asked.

Sam glanced at Amanda who nodded. "The Frisbee's back at the bench. I'll get it."

Sammy decided he didn't want to play, so Sam and Jack went off to entertain Chihuly—or vice versa—while Sammy sat on the bench beside Amanda. He stared straight ahead, legs swinging, saying nothing.

After a few moments, Amanda said, "You look even more like your dad in person than in the photos he's shown me. Do many people tell you that?"

"Yes."

"Does Jack look more like your mom?"

"I guess."

"And do I remember right that you're ten and Jack is seven?"

"Yes."

"Does this feel as awkward to you as it does to me?"

No response although she was sure she knew the answer.

"Okay, how about you ask the questions. Surely there's something you want to know about me." Amanda faced him, trying to read his expression.

"Are you going to marry my dad?" he asked without turning toward her.

"You don't mess around with the little stuff, do you? You are like your dad." She shook her head. "The answer is, we haven't talked about it. There are things that have to get settled first."

"Like what?"

"Well, the first one is, do his sons and I get along."

Sammy finally looked at her. "Jack will like you just because you have a dog."

"So you're the one I have to impress. Good to know." She smiled at him and got a half-smile back. Progress, she thought.

"Will you spend the weekends with us from now on when we're with Dad?" He'd turned away from her again.

"No, you guys don't have a lot of time together so I don't want to intrude. Although I wondered if you'd like to visit my studio sometime to see the two glassblowers I share space with work. I haven't said anything to your dad yet because I wanted to see if you were interested first."

"Dad said you're an artist."

"Yup. I work with glass but I don't blow it. The kind of work I do, you might be interested in doing yourself." As she went on to describe how she did her work, Sammy finally gave her his full attention.

*

It was killing Sam. He was trying to keep his mind on the Frisbee game but he really wanted to know what was going on with Amanda and Sammy. So far, Amanda was doing all the talking and his older son's face was set in a familiar stubborn expression.

Sammy was a hard sell. Jack had been so young when the divorce happened he barely noticed that his parents didn't live together any more. Sammy, on the other hand, had been old enough to be hurt and unhappy. He'd made it clear he wanted his parents back together. The first blow to his plans had been his mother's remarriage. Amanda, Sam knew, would be the last nail in the coffin, consigning his hopes for reconciliation to the flames.

Sam wanted this meeting to work out because he had his own plans. They included things he'd never believed in until recently, like sappy, "happily ever after" movie shit. And then there was this image that flashed through his mind of a little girl with his brown eyes and her caramel-colored curls, sitting in front of him on an Appaloosa, her fingers laced through his as they guided the horse around the corral at the family ranch.

All his plans depended on the woman on the bench. But before he could work on her about the plans, he had to know she and the boys were comfortable with each other.

Suddenly Sammy smiled at Amanda and started talking, his hands moving in explanation of something. Maybe he shouldn't have worried. She seemed to have charmed Sammy almost as fast as she'd charmed Sammy's father.

Sam signaled to Jack to wind down the game, and headed toward the bench, his younger son running before him.

Jack raced right to Amanda. "Dad said we could go to your house and have lunch and play with Chihuly some more. Is it really all right?"

She nodded.

"But Sammy has to want to go, too. Say yes, Sammy. Please?" Jack begged.

Amanda stood up. "How about I go clean up after my dog, who seems to have left a little present over there while you three decide?"

"No," Sammy said. "You don't have to leave. Going to your house for lunch is okay. And maybe we can go see your studio. Dad, Amanda says if you and Mom are cool with it, she'll teach us how to cut glass and make things like she does. Can we?"

Sam smiled at his son. "I'll talk to your mom and see what she says but, yeah, I think that sounds like a great idea. Today, though, we'll just watch Leo and Giles."

"I'll meet you there, Sam, as soon as I clean up after Chihuly," Amanda said. He nodded and kissed the top of her head.

"The guys blow glass, you know," Sammy said as they walked to where Sam's truck was parked. "Amanda does a different kind of glass art. She cuts up sheets of glass into designs and fuses them in a kiln." He continued, repeating almost word for word what Sam knew Amanda had told his son. Knew because she'd once explained it exactly like that to him.

*

That night, as he usually did after herding his sons to bed, Sam called Amanda, eager to find out how she felt about the day.

He broached the subject first. "You were a big hit. Not only is Jack in love with you because you have a dog, but you managed to charm Sammy, which is considerably harder. He says if I want to invite you for one of our Friday pizza nights or a Saturday green-eggs-and-ham dinner, it would be okay."

"You don't really make green eggs and ham, do you?"

"Close. When we eat in, we make odd combinations of food often dyed with a lot of food coloring to make up for the fact than none of the three of us can cook anything other than breakfast."

"I'm honored and scared, all at the same time."

"You're not only beautiful but wise." He was silent for a moment. "It went okay today, didn't it?"

"I think so. I hope so. I really liked your boys. Jack is adorable, so open and loving. And Sammy is so much like you it almost made me cry. You and your ex have done a great job raising them."

"Think you'd be okay with this more often, maybe even regularly?"

She hesitated a moment then said in a soft voice, "Yeah, I think I would."

In that admission, he heard the first sign that she might be ready to talk about some of his plans for their future.

*

The plan was moving but not fast enough. The money hadn't panned out yet. Turned out, getting into the bitch's house wasn't easy, between the security system, the dog, and the fucking cop who was almost living there. By convincing that idiot Kane he'd be better off letting the lawyers work it out, he'd slowed down one half of the operation while he kept trying to get around the complications.

Lucky he had this bolthole. No one knew he kipped here except the owner, a guy he met last year who was still away. The place was a pile of shit, hardly any furniture, bad plumbing, no electricity. But using this place got him out from under the supervision of the people who were keeping track of him. He needed to get away sometimes, so he didn't get squirrely.

The whole thing was making him crazy. All he heard was how important patience and persistence were. Fuck that. He was running out of both. One last try to get in the house and he'd force the issue with phase two. He'd make her pay for the murder she'd gotten away with. And when they locked her up, he'd be able to find what he was looking for and leave town. This waiting was getting on his nerves.

Chapter Seven

"Where've you been?" Eubie Kane asked. He was standing outside the door of the now closed and darkened Bullseye Resource Center, shivering in the fall rain. Next to him was a hand truck piled with plastic tubs. "Why'd you keep me waiting so long?"

"I couldn't do anything until Robin went across the way to set up for her class," the man holding open the door said.

"Yeah, *her* class. She's a second-rate teacher. I'd do better." Kane wheeled his hand truck toward the classroom area. The other man closed and locked the front door.

"Whatever." The man shrugged, bored with listening to the young artist's complaints. "She said it would be about an hour. So that's what you have to get that thing set up so it'll start doing whatever it does after we leave."

"You mean program the controller so the kiln fires my work overnight," Kane said in a patronizing tone. The other man barely controlled his impulse to punch the artist in the mouth.

Apparently oblivious to the reaction he was causing, Kane went on. "I called Amanda St. Claire. I'm going to her studio when I'm finished here. I've talked to my lawyer and have a figure to give her. She's going to freak when I tell her how much it'll cost her to keep me from taking her to court." He pried the lid off the top bin and unpacked pieces of art glass swathed in bubble-wrap. He carefully removed the plastic and placed the glass on the worktables in the middle of the room.

"She said she thought it would be a good idea for us to get together. I bet she thinks she can talk her way out of this." The artist grinned at the man he thought was his buddy. "But when I'm finished with her, she'll be sorry she took advantage of me.

And once I'm recognized for what I am—an artist who inspires other artists—I'll be able to pay you back for the money you loaned me for the lawyer."

"Nah, that was a gift from another friend. Don't worry. You deserve what you're gonna get."

Eubie rearranged the stacks of glass on the table as he talked. "I owe you a lot more than money. I've been struggling for years to be taken seriously. Your ideas have been inspired. First suing Amanda. Then confronting Liz. Now having the staff here awed by a kiln load of my new pieces. Finally, I'm catching a break . . . "

Kane droned on and the other man zoned out, lounging on the lowest tier of the stadium seating where students usually watched artist demonstrations. Thank Christ he'd overheard Eubie bitching about artists using his ideas when he was with Robin in the coffee shop. With very little persuasion Eubie began to believe that the St. Claire bitch was one of them. Eubie was so perfect for the plan it was almost scary.

He watched Kane finish unwrapping the last of fifteen pieces of glass with minimal designs on each one. "Whadda you call your work, Eubie?" he asked. "I forget."

"The old work you saw was weather moods. The new work is seasonal moods." He held up a stack of fired eight-inch squares. "You can see how different it is."

The man on the steps couldn't but what the hell.

"This one is the first of the series." Eubie spread out a clear glass square with a tan foreground, a square with white hills and a third piece with a faint shadow of a mountain. "It's called 'Winter on the Mountain.' Then I have 'Fall in the Gorge' and 'Summer in the . . . ' "

"Can I do anything to help you get this done?" he interrupted.

"Sure, you can clean the pieces. I have cleaning solution and towels here."

"Doesn't Bullseye have something? Why waste your money when we can waste theirs?"

Eubie grinned and retrieved a white towel with thin red stripes and a spray bottle from under a nearby worktable. The man took the supplies and squirted the contents of the spray bottle on a piece of glass, paying more attention to the young artist than to his task.

"So, all you have to do is punch in those numbers and the kiln does the rest of the work?"

"Yes," Eubie answered, "once I've entered the firing schedule, all those numbers as you call it, all I have to do is hit the 'start' button and the kiln takes it from there."

When the man was sure Kane had returned his attention to the kiln, he noiselessly put the piece of glass back on the workbench, pulled a pair of latex gloves from his jeans, put them on, and eased a small handgun out of a jacket pocket.

Kane was just finishing double-checking the firing schedule when the man grabbed him around the throat. Eubie made a gagging sound and dropped the paper he'd been holding as he struggled to relieve the pressure on his neck. But the slender artist was no match for a man who had worked out religiously in a prison exercise yard and in his apartment in preparation for this moment.

"Relax, Eubie. I'm about to make you more famous than you could get with that shit you call art. And we'll make that little bitch pay, like you want, like we both want."

Holding the young artist with his right arm he hit him in the head with the gun then pushed him to the floor. He shot the stunned Kane in the head. After watching the artist bleed out what was left of his life onto the cement floor, the man dropped the gun next to the body and began to look around to see what he needed to tidy up. He saw Eubie's glass. What the fuck, he thought, might as well finish it. Give Eubie one last chance at glory. If he got it done quickly, he could get across to where Robin was before she came to him.

But after he transferred Kane's work into the kiln in the order he thought it went, there was space left. He looked around to see if he'd missed more work. "Fucking idiot," he muttered, "I give him his shot at using this thing and he doesn't even fill it." Although there was no more of Kane's work, on another table sat four stacks of glass with a note on top that said, "Fire for Amanda St. Claire."

"Sweet," he said under his breath and filled the rest of the space in the large kiln with a few pieces of Amanda's work. "The two of them together will be a nice touch."

When he'd finished, he made two quick phone calls. As he was about to close and start the kiln, the door from the delivery area opened.

"Hey, sweet cheeks, I finished early so let's blow this Popsicle stand and get dinner." Robin Jordan stopped, looked at the open kiln. "What the hell is going on in here? Why're you messing around with the big kiln?" She walked toward her boyfriend, saw Eubie Kane's body on the floor and stopped. Her eyes widened, she took a deep, sharp breath, the expression on her face moving from curiosity to horror. "What happened here?" She looked up at him. "That wasn't a backfire noise I heard a while ago, was it?"

He reached for her. "I'm sorry about this, Robin, but it looks like there isn't any other way. Waste of a good fuck, too."

She backed away from him, made a break for the retail area. He chased her, snagged her arm, and stopped her.

"Let me go, goddamn it. What are you doing?" she yelled, scratching at his face. He recoiled, which gave her a second chance to run. But he was faster. Grabbing her, his hand clamped over her mouth, he dragged her toward the classroom.

She kicked and bit; his grip loosened enough for her to come at him again with her nails. He put his hands up to protect his face so all she was able to do was snag one of the latex gloves, ripping it and scratching his hand. He backed up, knocking over a display of frit, sending the jars of granulated glass rolling in all directions. He stumbled on one and cursed.

Robin grabbed a wooden box packed with a couple dozen five-by-ten inch samples of glass and swung it at him. He deflected the blow and knocked the box out of her hand, tearing the second glove on the rough wooden crate and cutting his hand. The contents crashed to the floor, shards of glass scattering in all directions.

Finally he got his arms around her torso, overpowered her, and smashed her head against a pedestal. Stunned, she was barely struggling as he dragged her back into the classroom. He hit her again before dumping her face down on top of Eubie Kane's body. Grabbing the blood-streaked towel next to Kane's body, he used it to pick up the handgun. He dispatched Robin in the same way he had the young artist.

Satisfied she was dead, he dropped the gun beside the two bodies and stripped off what was left of the gloves. He closed the lid to the kiln, hit the button Kane had indicated, and doused the one light they had turned on. In the dark, he edged his way toward the front door, the gloves and towel in his hand.

Before he got there he heard someone rattling the front door from outside. A familiar face peered in through the glass. Still in shadow, he paused. As soon as the woman disappeared, he started again toward the door.

But the sound of men's voices coming from the ramp leading to the warehouse and factory stopped him. Reversing directions, he retreated to the classroom. For what seemed like forever but was probably only five or six minutes, he waited by the door to the delivery area, listening to what was happening in the other part of the building.

Two men had come up from the factory. Using a flashlight to rake dark corners, they moved toward the front door. Then one of them stumbled on a jar of frit and they both crunched across the broken glass. They turned on overhead lights, cursed, and called nine-one-one.

The man in the classroom waited until he was sure they were absorbed in reporting the incident before he noiselessly opened the door and left the building by way of the delivery entrance. The woman who'd banged at the front was standing on the sidewalk when he got outside, backlit from a powerful security light at the business across the street. Hoping to frighten her away, he pointed at her, as if he had a gun. She ran.

When he thought she had driven off, he went to his car and left. It hadn't gone exactly the way he'd planned it, but it was done. There was only one more thing and he'd be finished for the evening.

*

Sam Richardson and his new partner Danny Hartmann caught the case. They were to meet at the Bullseye Resource Center where two bodies had just been found by night staff. It would be their first homicide working together.

When he walked in to the place he'd only heard about from Amanda, Sam's attention was not immediately drawn, as it usually was, to the yellow crime scene tape. Instead what he saw was Amanda's studio on steroids.

Glass was everywhere—stacked, stored, shelved, and smashed. Along the south wall were slots of plywood housing sheets of glass in more colors than he knew existed. Each slot was topped with a small, backlit sample of the color, giving that side of the room a border of jewel-like intensity. Hundreds of jars of frit were stacked in bookcase-type shelves. Bricks of glass sat on low display tables, finished objects on pedestals. The shattered pieces on the floor and the police officers combing through them brought him back to why he was there.

Over the next few hours he and his partner interviewed the owners and the security guards who had called nine-one-one. They talked with the crime scene technicians and cops going over the two areas in a grid search trying to find anything that looked like evidence.

By the time the ME took the bodies for autopsy, Sam and his partner knew what little anyone was sure of: First, the security system had been disarmed a few minutes before 8:30 pm using Robin Jordan's code. Jordan, an employee in the company's Research and Education Department, was one of the victims. Second, materials had been set out for a class Jordan was scheduled to teach in the morning in a classroom across the delivery entrance from the murder scene. Those preparations were, everyone assumed, why she had been there. Third, something had happened after she set it up to cause a hell of a fight in the retail store and result in two dead bodies.

That's where the facts ended and the questions began. There were no signs of forced entry any place in the rest of the complex. Nothing seemed missing. Since Robin Jordan had disarmed the security system and was one of the victims, did the killer make her open the building? But if the killer had forced her to open the building, why hadn't she hit the silent alarm? And if she let the killer in, why did she just go about setting up her classroom? Did she know her killer? Her car wasn't there. How had she gotten to Bullseye?

And why was Eubie Kane there? A van registered to him was parked out front and a hand-truck with his name on it stacked with empty plastic bins was near where the bodies had been found. Was he there with Jordan? Had he brought her there? Was one the target and the other just unlucky enough to be in the wrong place? If so, which was which? And why did anyone want to kill either of them?

More questions than answers. As usual.

Chapter Eight

Early next morning Sam returned to southeast Portland to familiarize himself with the neighborhood around Bullseye. Walking the block, he saw the retail store/classroom facility was only a small portion of the operation. The factory, where the glass was made, took up most of the space.

Although the retail store was closed while the police continued their investigation, the owners showed up early, too, to be on hand to answer more questions for the police, their employees and to cancel classes for the day. They brought coffee and scones and made space available on the second floor overlooking the murder site so Sam and his partner could continue their interviews.

The detectives asked each person about any possible problems Eubie Kane and Robin Jordan had recently had. Little they heard about the young instructor helped. She was single with no local family, loved her job, and was a good teacher and a skilled artist. She seemed to have no enemies.

Only two interesting pieces of information surfaced. The first was that recently she'd been wearing an expensive-looking gold bracelet. Sam had seen it on her body, another sign, he thought, that the motive for the murders was not robbery. One of her colleagues thought it was a gift from her new boyfriend—the second piece of information. Robin had been secretive about him, not wanting to jinx the budding relationship, she said. The only thing the woman who reported it knew was Robin had met him at a nearby coffee shop about two or three months before.

Eubie Kane was quite a different story. If he didn't have enemies, he didn't have many friends either. Described by more than one person as petulant and over-sensitive, his only connection with

Robin Jordan seemed to be that he'd been in a couple of her classes. Robin's friends laughed at the idea he might be her new boyfriend, saying he wasn't her type and he certainly couldn't afford that gold bracelet.

Since a good portion of the staff working the retail store had been witness to it, both detectives heard versions of Kane's confrontation with Amanda St. Claire. Most of it tracked what Amanda had told Sam weeks before—for no reason anyone could figure out, Kane had threatened to sue her for stealing his ideas.

Last, they heard about Kane having a run-in with a gallery owner. Everyone assumed it was the owner of one of the two galleries where he showed his work: The Fairchild Gallery in Portland or He Sells Seashells, at the coast.

Leaving his partner to finish up the interviews, Sam returned to Central Precinct where he found waiting for him the list of what had been in Eubie Kane's pockets and Robin Jordan's purse. The only thing interesting was from Kane's pocket—a piece of paper torn in two on which the words *"Not only no but hell no"* were written. The message was on the back of a piece of brown paper on which there was part of a shipping label. Sam called the gallery on the label but got voice mail. He left a message asking for a return call.

A report on the fingerprints on the weapon found with the bodies, which was also on his desk, was more problematic.

Sam knocked on the open door to Christopher Angel's office. The lieutenant in charge of the homicide detectives in Central Precinct was on the phone but signaled Sam in and waved him to a chair while he wrapped up the conversation.

A fifty-six-year-old, tall, slim man with dark hair shot through with the white he swore came from parenting five daughters rather than his work, Angel had been in his job for four years. His solve rate was impressive, the press loved him, and the Chief relied on his impeccable instincts about both homicide and public relations. His detectives had a nickname for him—L.T. The casual use of the initials was less about their recognition of his rank than a sign of their regard for him.

"Sorry to keep you waiting," he said as he hung up. That was the Chief passing along a message from the mayor. Mr. Mayor wants Kane/Jordan cleared quickly so it doesn't, and I'm quoting here, 'give the business community the impression that it's not safe to operate in Portland.' The fact that two people are dead apparently didn't enter into their conversation." He shrugged his shoulders and shook his head, his disgusted look indicating exactly what he thought about the interchange. "What've you got for me?"

Sam ran down the list of the evidence they'd collected: The handgun they'd found next to the bodies. Shreds of latex gloves spotted with blood discovered in the parking area. The contents of Kane's pockets and Jordan's purse. The list of phone calls to and from both victims' cell phones.

"And there's this." Sam handed a lab report to Angel. "They lifted prints from the gun before it was sent for testing. There were partials on the barrel, nothing on the rest of it, a different set on the remaining cartridges. The partials were identified as Amanda St. Claire's. No match yet for the other set."

"Amanda St. Claire? I know that name." Angel paused for a moment. "Oh, shit, the goddamn Webster case. I hoped I'd never hear any name from that case again," he said, almost growling.

Sam shook his head, wishing like hell he didn't have to say what he was about to say. "If you'll look on that list of phone calls you'll see Kane made a call to St. Claire's number early in the evening. And there was an incoming call from her phone later, after he was dead."

"I hate to ask—does she have a connection with Kane?"

"Other than the fact both are glass artists, yeah. He caused a scene in Bullseye recently, accusing her of stealing his designs. Threatened her with a lawsuit." He shifted uneasily in the chair.

"She also heard that Kane was trolling the DA's office to see who'd bite on his story about intellectual property theft."

"When you talked to her about this did you find out where she was last night?"

"Haven't talked to her yet."

"Then how do you know the details of her dispute with Kane?"

"That's why I came to see you as soon as I found out about the fingerprints and phone calls. I think I need to get off this case. We're involved. Amanda and I, that is. She told me about her Kane problem when it happened."

"*Think* you need to get off? Jesus Christ, Sam, of course you're off. How much of the evidence has your name on it?"

"None. Danny and one of the uniforms took care of that. I did interviews."

Angel fiddled with a pen for a moment, then stood up. "Does Danny have the addresses of St. Claire's home and studio or wherever she works?"

"Not sure." He broke eye contact with the lieutenant.

"The way you answered that tells me there's something else I'm not going to like. Is it where she lives or where she works that's making you nervous?"

"She lives in Alameda. Her studio is in southeast Portland, about half a mile from Bullseye."

"Shit. Shit. Shit." Angel bounced the pen off the top of his desk. "We have a possible motive for St. Claire, she may have been nearby, and her fingerprints are on the murder weapon."

"I'm sure there's an explanation. "

"You won't be the one finding it." He paused, forcing Sam to look at him by the power of the silence. "You're not on leave like last year. You're working for me. And you're off this case." There was another long, hard silence. "Am I clear here?"

"Got it, L.T.," Sam said.

*

It had been a terrible morning for Amanda. She'd started out sleep deprived after a restless night. Then the news this morning. Then when she got to her studio she found they'd been broken into, for the second time in a week. The first time the desk in the office had been rifled. This time it was more like last year when Tom Webster had trashed a year's worth of her work because he'd discovered she'd found evidence of the drug-dealing going on in his club.

Whoever broke in the night before, however, had made no distinction between her work and that of her studio mates. Thousands of dollars of finished or almost completed work as well as hundreds and hundreds of dollars worth of sheet glass had been smashed and heaped in a huge pile in the middle of the studio.

But there was something worse in the office. Thank God she was there first because on the desk, in an envelope addressed to her, was a note from the person who broke into the studio.

The same person she'd seen the night before at Bullseye.

He said that if she didn't keep her mouth shut, there would be consequences for her and for "her cop." He also enclosed a copy of a letter signed by Tom Webster and addressed to "Buddy." Before she could read the second letter, however, Giles and Leo arrived. She jammed the letters back into the envelope and went out to join them in the outrage about what had happened. Once they'd vented about it, they began the cleanup.

An hour later, Amanda looked up from sweeping to see a strange woman standing in the middle of the GlassCo studio. Tall and fit looking, her dark blonde hair was cut in a short, attractive wash-and-wear style. Dressed in navy blue trousers, a white scoop neck knit shirt, and a lightweight blue and white tweed jacket, she held a zippered leather case the size of a file folder and projected the message that she expected to own any room she entered.

Amanda wasn't sure how long the woman had been there. With

loud music playing and the noise of sweeping up and dumping piles of glass, the sound of the door opening or the woman's heels had been lost. The stranger could have been there for a long time, just watching. She looked like that's what she was up to, just watching.

"Can I help you?" Amanda asked.

"Amanda St. Claire?" Without waiting for an answer, the woman said, "I'm Danny Hartmann." She flipped out a badge. "Detective Danny Hartmann."

"Sam's new partner? I didn't know . . . "

" . . . I was a woman? Easy mistake. Danny seemed like a better name for a cop than either Danita or Rebecca, the choices my mother gave me." Hartmann paused for a few seconds longer than Amanda liked, looking around. "I'd like to talk to you. Is there someplace private we can go?"

Amanda felt her eyes widen and the blood leave her head. "Oh, God, something's happened to Sam, hasn't it?" She held onto the broom she'd been using with a death grip hoping it would hold her up if this woman had come to tell her that the consequences of what she'd seen the night before had already played out.

"No, nothing like that. Sam's fine. I just need to talk to you."

As the tension left her body, Amanda felt herself deflate. "Then he didn't—" She stopped to take a deep breath. "Right. Talk. We can go in the back." She propped the broom against a table before leading the detective to the office.

"What's going on out there?" Hartmann asked as she sat in the chair Amanda offered.

"Someone broke in last night. Second time in a week. This time it's a freaking disaster—an expensive, freaking disaster. And there was . . . " she let it trail off and broke eye contact with Hartmann. She realized she was playing with the envelope that held the two letters. Not sure yet what she was going to do about them, she did know she didn't want Detective Hartmann getting curious so she slid the envelope from the desktop into a partially open desk drawer and closed it.

"You report it to the police?"

Amanda looked up, wondering how Hartmann knew about the letters, then realized that wasn't what she meant. "Oh, the break-in? Yeah, I guess I should. Usually it's . . . you know . . . just addicts looking for money although this seems different. More like the time my work got destroyed last year. But, I'll worry about it later. What is it you wanted to talk about?"

"Eubie Kane. You heard he was killed last night."

Amanda took a sharp breath. "Yes . . . I . . . ah . . . heard it on the radio this morning and saw it in the paper. Eubie and poor Robin." She looked away from the other woman, biting her lip, picked up a pen and clicked the cap off and on a few times before quickly looking back at the detective.

"Eubie called me last night and asked to come over here to see me. But he never showed up. I didn't know why until I . . . until this morning when I heard the news." She slid back in her chair. "Why do you want to talk to me about him?"

Without answering, Hartmann brought a photograph out of her leather bag. "Do you recognize this?"

Amanda took the photo, looked at it for a moment and shook her head. "It's a gun. Should it mean something to me?" She looked at the photo a second time before handing it back to the detective. "One of my studio mates keeps something that looks like it in the desk for protection."

"We found this next to the bodies. It's being tested to see if it's the murder weapon but I'm assuming it is. It's registered to a Leo Wilson. Is that the name of your studio mate?"

Amanda stifled a gasp. She nodded. Barely.

"Your fingerprints are on the barrel."

"*My* fingerprints? How?" She moved in the chair as if the place she was sitting had suddenly warmed up. "The only time I even touch it is to move it out of the way when I go into his drawer. Leo's drawer is the only one with a lock of sorts on it so we keep petty cash there and the stamps."

"A lock of sorts?"

"You can open the drawer with a knife. Maybe even a paper clip."

"When did you see his gun last?"

"See it? A week or so ago."

"When was the last break-in, did you say?"

"I didn't. It was about four days ago."

Hartmann paused to write a few things down in a notebook. Then she looked up and asked, "Where were you last night between say, seven and ten?"

"I was mostly here." Amanda moved restlessly again. "Mostly alone. Leo and Giles left about seven. I was working on pieces I wanted to fire today after I unloaded the kilns this morning so I stayed late."

"Did you see or talk to anyone while you were here?"

Amanda sat up straight and squared her shoulders. "Eubie called me about seven, I think. Leo was gone. Giles was still here. Eubie asked to meet with me. I told him I would be in my studio until about ten and he was welcome to come talk to me."

"Giles—which one is he?"

"The blond. Leo's the dark-haired one."

"And he was here when Kane called?"

Amanda nodded. "I was talking to him, planning what we were going to do with kilns for the next couple of days. My cell rang and I took the call."

"I heard Kane accused you of stealing from him. Why'd you agree to meet him?"

"I figured it couldn't hurt to try to settle this thing between us. But I finished earlier than I expected. I called him. Told him I was going home. I got voice mail and left a message." She picked up the pen again and played with it.

"I'll need a statement from you about what you did yesterday. Want to do that now?" Hartmann asked.

Amanda hesitated for a moment. "Well, I have all that mess out there, but okay. The mess will be here when I get back."

Giles interrupted. "Amanda, can I talk to you for a minute?"

"Sure, what's up?"

"I think we better do this privately." He cut his eyes toward the detective.

Amanda shook her head. "Whatever it is, let's get it out in the open."

He produced a neatly folded white towel with red stripes and dark splotches of what looked like dried blood on it. "I found this under that big pile of broken glass."

"That's not one of our towels," Amanda said.

"No," Giles said, "it looks like the ones Bullseye instructors use to clean glass in the classroom." He carefully unfolded the towel. Inside was a clip of bullets. "This was wrapped in it. It looks like the one for Leo's gun. How do you think . . . ?"

Hartmann interrupted. "You found a clip you believe came from Leo Wilson's gun in a Bullseye towel here?" She stood up and reached for the towel. "I'll take it. I want to talk to you and Leo, too. Will you be here for a while? Amanda and I are going to the precinct. Should be back in a couple hours."

"I'm here until seven. I'll make sure Leo doesn't leave until you talk to him."

*

When Amanda and Detective Hartmann returned to the GlassCo studio from Central Precinct, there was an urgent message from Felicia Hamilton at Bullseye. Felicia had opened the big Paragon kiln. Instead of the sample pieces for Robin Jordan's class she expected to find, she discovered what might have been Eubie

Kane's work. "Might have been" meaning that it had been laid up incorrectly and was ruined, but Hamilton thought she recognized it as Eubie's work from what remained. Unfortunately, some of Amanda's work may have been involved, too.

Although she tried to get out of it, Amanda accompanied Detective Hartmann to Bullseye. She hung back near the worktables at the center of the room, trying not to look at the crime scene tape still in place, while the detective and Felicia Hamilton peered into what looked, to the uninitiated, like a cross between a coffin and a tanning bed. Inside the kiln was a large piece of glass completely covering the surface of the shelves. Glassy icicles hung from the sides of the shelves and the bottom of the kiln was dotted with glass puddles.

"So, tell me in language I'll understand what happened here," Hartmann said.

Felicia said, "Whoever laid up this glass in the kiln—put the work on the shelves—didn't know how to do it. Assuming this was Eubie's, his work is nine to twelve millimeters thick. Glass holds its shape at the temperatures we fire to if it's six millimeters thick. Any thicker and it flows out as it becomes molten, trying to even out to six millimeters. So, when we fire a project that's designed to be thicker, we use dams and bricks to contain it while it fuses and cools. Whoever put the glass in here didn't do that. Eubie, of course, would have."

"So, you're saying that Kane didn't put the glass on the shelves."

"I don't think so. But the controller," Felicia pointed to a box with three rows of buttons on the side of the kiln, "that automatically raises and lowers the temperature of the kiln, seems to have been programmed correctly. If it hadn't been, the glass wouldn't have fused and cooled without thermal shocking, breaking from changes in temperatures. Glass doesn't handle temperature changes easily."

"Kane?" asked Hartmann.

"Just guessing, but I'd say, yes. And this morning I was asked to identify a piece of paper one of your officers found under another kiln," Felicia said. "It looked like a firing schedule." She answered the question before the detective could ask it. "The directions for the controller. It looked like a firing schedule for thick blocks like Eubie's and it was in what looked like Eubie's handwriting. He always makes—always *made*—his sevens like European ones with a cross on them and made little curls on his zeros."

Hartmann looked back into the open kiln. "So Kane's work was wrecked."

"And apparently two pieces of mine." Amanda had moved closer to the kiln and finally spoke. "Yesterday I left four pieces on that workstation over there to be fired when a kiln was available. I rent space here when all our kilns are in use. There are only two pieces left over there. If the person who loaded the kiln knew what they were doing, Eubie's work, along with the dams and bricks supporting it, would have filled the shelves. Looks like whoever did this piled in Eubie's work and used my stuff to take up the remaining space."

Hartmann looked to Felicia. "So, the kiln was loaded wrong but programmed right."

Felicia nodded.

Amanda's curiosity had gotten the better of her and she was inspecting the piece in the kiln. "If you need more proof that whoever did this doesn't understand glass, look at this." She pointed to marks on the surface of the glass. "That looks like fingerprints." The manager pulled her glasses down from the top of her head, looked carefully at the glass and agreed.

"Fingerprints? You mean the glass shows fingerprints even after it's fired?" Hartmann asked.

"It can. Don't know if you could convict someone on the basis of what's left but it's clear enough to screw up a project. That's part of the reason we clean pieces so carefully before we fire them.

Whoever put this in here didn't do that," Felicia said as she reached to pull at the piece of glass.

"Don't touch it," Hartmann said. She pulled out her cell phone. "I'm calling the crime scene guys back to process it as evidence." Inspecting the glass piece she asked, "How big would you say this sucker is?"

"The shelves measure twenty-six by fifty-two inches," Felicia said. "How long will it take to get this kiln freed up? One of the techs will have to dig all that glass out of the bricks in the bottom before we can use it again."

"Sorry, but don't count on having access to it for a while." When she finished the phone call, Hartmann turned to Amanda. "Let's go back to your studio. We need to talk some more."

*

After Danny Hartmann left the studio, Amanda went to the back office and shut the door, telling her studio mates she had to work on the books and asked them not to interrupt. But it wasn't account books she pulled out of the desk drawer. It was the envelope left by the intruder. This time she carefully read both letters. The one she'd already read was a clear threat. But the other one, a copy of a letter from Tom Webster, seemed to explain why someone was trying to get into her house.

She had to think this through. Figure out what to do. She pulled out her phone to call Sam. He'd know.

Wait. That's exactly what the first letter said not to do. If she called Sam, she put him in danger. Maybe she could just tell him about the second letter. But how would she explain how she got it? And why she didn't tell his partner about it.

Until she decided what to do, she'd take them both home and lock them in her desk there. If she hadn't figured it out by the time the police solved the murders, she'd turn the letters over to them.

They wouldn't be happy but surely they'd understand why she did it. Wouldn't they?

Funny, last year, she didn't trust the Police Bureau to detect their way out of a gunnysack. This year, she had to depend on them to find out who this guy was. And fast. Until they did, she had to protect Sam the way he'd protected her. She didn't know how good she would be at lying to him. It was hard enough keeping what she knew from Danny Hartmann.

It had been a great relief when she realized Sam wasn't around when she'd been at the precinct. If she'd had to go through that conversation with Detective Hartmann in front of him, she'd have never been able to keep anything secret.

Oh, God, it was last year all over again. The threat from Eubie Kane. Now his murder. Her prints on Leo's gun. A gun found at the murder scene. Her wrecked studio. She was being set up for something she hadn't done. And the next step was for no one to believe her and . . .

No, she wouldn't go there. She'd just see how it unfolded. Maybe it would be different this time.

*

Two hours after she got home that night, Sam appeared at her door.

"You must wonder about your luck," she said when he took her in his arms. "How many men have women in their lives who are constantly suspected of murdering people?"

"Amanda, no one thinks . . . "

"Yes, they do. Don't b.s. me." She turned her face up to him, hoping he didn't see what was underlying her fear.

"We'll find the person who did this and it'll be fine."

"I can't go through this again, I can't." She buried her face in his shirt and wept.

When she'd stopped crying, he led her to the living room couch. He wiped her eyes with his handkerchief. "Tell me about yesterday."

"I went to work at noon. I came home a little after nine. It was just the usual."

"What about the phone call from Eubie Kane?"

"What about it? He called and asked if he could meet me at the studio. I told him he was welcome to come by before ten."

"Why would you do that?"

"I thought we could get it straightened out. But he never showed. So, before I came home I called him to say I was leaving. He didn't answer."

"That's all there was?"

"Why do you keep asking me questions? You don't think I did this, do you?"

"Of course not. I'm only trying to work out what happened."

"Are you and Detective Hartmann assigned to this?"

He avoided looking at her as he answered. "No, I've been . . . Danny's working it."

"So, you're out of it." She ran her fingers through her hair and stared at the ceiling so he couldn't see that she was pleased he had been taken off the case.

"It doesn't mean I'm not interested." He gently tipped her face down so she was looking at him. "I'm trying to figure out why the killer went to the trouble of stealing that specific gun to use on a guy who came out of nowhere riled up about you. Doesn't that seem strange to you?"

She teared up again.

Sam kissed her forehead. "Okay, that's enough. Let's change the subject. How about I have a pizza delivered and stay with you tonight?"

"I'd love it, to all three suggestions. Thank you." She wiped her eyes and started to get up. "I better go take care of Chihuly."

"I'll do that after I call for the pizza. Your usual Margherita?"

*

They went to bed early. Unlike most nights when they slept together, Amanda had donned a light cotton nightgown. It was convent-modest; the last thing on her mind was sex. But when she curled up in a ball clutching her pillow, Sam lay down beside her, still dressed, and slowly, rhythmically, rubbed her shoulders to relax her. In only a few minutes, she began to respond to him just as she always did, her nipples hardening, her breathing kicking up a notch or two.

She shrugged her shoulder up, turned her head, kissed his hand, then faced him. He whispered, "Good night" and moved to kiss her softly but she took his mouth in what was no tentative goodnight peck but a fierce, demanding kiss. Her lips parted, her tongue urged his mouth to open for her.

He broke from their embrace. "Amanda, don't you think you'd do better with some sleep?"

"Please, Sam, I need you tonight."

"Oh, baby, you always have me, you know that." He pulled her closer, kissed her tenderly, skating his hands over her back.

She broke free to unbutton his shirt. He began to help but she brushed his hands away. "Let me. Tonight, let me do this."

When she'd finished unbuttoning his shirt, he shed it, then pulled off his boots before he lay back down again. He watched as she opened the zipper on his jeans then worked them off along with his boxer briefs.

After she'd finished undressing him, she knelt between his legs looking at what she'd uncovered—his powerful thighs, the erection she had plans for, the chest and shoulders she loved to touch. When she shed her nightgown she accidently brushed it across his penis. Sam groaned as his member jumped in response to the light touch. She loved seeing how much he wanted her, how he needed this as much as she did tonight.

Running her hands up his thighs, she avoided touching his erection, instead caressing his abs and his chest. When she reached his face, she leaned in, felt him press his hips up against her, heard him groan again, but she buried the sound in a kiss.

He lifted her hips up to bring her sex in contact with his but she fought it, moving back down his body. With hot, wet, lingering kisses she covered his neck, his chest, his navel while her hand found its way to his penis. Rubbing him, feeling the strength and power of his erection made her wet and needy. But she wanted to do something for him first, something that would make her feel in control of some aspect of her life.

On her knees again, she moved her mouth to join her hand and took him in, a bit at a time, sucking, licking. Listening to him groan as she continued to stroke and suck stoked her desire. She loved the taste of him, the taste of salt and sex and the sea. She could have gone on for hours.

But he couldn't. He reached down for her, pulled her up and handed her a condom. She quickly covered him and positioned herself over him so he could enter her. When he drove into her, he obliterated any thought from her mind other than how good it felt to have him fill her. With only a few powerful thrusts, they both reached climax.

Wordlessly she collapsed on him and he held her. When she tried to hide the tears leaking from her eyes, he didn't say anything, only kissed each one. As they lay there, bodies still entwined, Amanda wondered if this time even Sam could ward off the ghosts she could feel gathering outside in the dusk.

*

Early the next morning before the alarm went off Amanda wakened with an uneasy feeling. She listened for a sound that was out of the ordinary, tried to remember if she'd had a bad dream. When she was fully awake, it all came back to her. What had happened. What she knew. What she had to hide. Even though she was wrapped in a blanket, she began to shiver and couldn't stop, waking Sam with her shaking.

He reached for her. "Cold, baby?"

"Scared." She crept into his arms.

"We'll work this out. It's not the same as . . . " He didn't finish the sentence. "How 'bout we go to the beach this weekend? We can rent horses from your friend's stable and I'll let you beat me in a race on the beach. Or, we can go to the movies and you can pick a sappy romantic movie and make me watch it. Or . . . "

She put her hand over his mouth. "Don't, Sam, please. I'm not in the mood for joking."

He kissed her. "I was going to say, or we could make love again."

"Not this morning, Sam." She grabbed the quilt that had drifted down to the foot of the bed and wrapped herself in it, turning her back on him. He tried to hold her but she hugged the edge of the bed on her side.

Chapter Nine

Sam was off the case but he wasn't out of the loop. He picked up gossip from colleagues and his partner shared what she could. When all else failed, he snooped.

Danny Hartman told him Amanda's supposed motive was proving to be weak. No one in the art community had heard of—or believed—Kane's assertion that she stole ideas from him. Everyone thought it was just a jealous artist shooting off his mouth. Not only would Kane have lost in court, he'd have lost everyone's respect because he'd tried to ruin a talented and well-liked artist.

Among the police investigating the murders, there was serious doubt that Amanda could have dragged Robin Jordan back to the classroom after the struggle evident in the retail area. And the ME's report looked good. Sam had seen it sitting on Danny's desk and had read it. He didn't think she'd mind.

It said that, from the bruising on Kane's neck and the angle of the gunshot wound, it was probable a left-handed person had wrestled the six-foot, three-inch victim to the ground before shooting him. Amanda was right-handed, more than foot shorter and weighed less than the bales of hay he'd bucked on the ranch.

And from the scrapings under her fingernails, Jordan had scratched her assailant. Amanda showed no signs of scratches.

By the time he'd finished reading the report, Sam could almost believe it was all over. Amanda was home free. He'd be back on the case with Danny and they would turn their attention to looking for the real perp.

Then he was called into L.T.'s office. Danny was there. When she avoided his gaze he knew it wasn't going to be a good conversation.

After the usual throat-clearing preliminaries were out of the way, Angel said, "I need to ask you a few questions about Amanda St. Claire. You comfortable with that?"

"I guess."

"What'd she tell you about the break-in at her studio the night of the murders?"

Sam relaxed back in the chair. Maybe this wouldn't be so bad after all. Maybe they were just cleaning up the details. "Just that it happened. It's not the first time. Not even the first time this month. That building's as easy to get into as a pop-top can."

"Yeah, she said. Did she tell you anything else about it?"

"You mean the bloody towel and the clip from Leo's gun? Yeah." He looked at the lieutenant, trying to figure out where this conversation was headed. "Don't you think it was the killer trying to throw suspicion on her? I do."

"What else did she say about the night of the murder?"

"Nothing. Is there something she should have told me?"

The lieutenant nodded to Danny.

Still avoiding Sam's eyes, she said, "There was a guy working late across the street from Bullseye. A little after nine, he was loading up his truck when he saw a red SUV pull into the parking area in front of the Resource Center. It was raining so he didn't get a clear look at the plate but he thought it was a vanity plate with no numbers."

Sam jumped out of his chair and began to walk back and forth across the office.

Danny continued. "A short woman got out of the vehicle, went to the front door. Then she ran south, along Twenty-first, toward the factory entrance. He was pulling out less than ten minutes later when he saw her come around the corner from the north side of the building, like a bat out of hell, he said. She got in the SUV and roared out." She caught Sam's arm as he paced past her. "He saw the first and last letters in the plate as she pulled out. They were G and O. Amanda drives . . . "

"A two-year-old red Toyota Highlander with a plate that says 'GLASSCO.'" Sam finished her sentence as he shook off her hand.

"Amanda was there, Sam, around the time of the murders. The question is, why does she think she has to lie about it?"

"Christ," Sam muttered as he continued to pace around the room, his hands jammed into his jeans' pockets. "What the hell did she think . . . ?" He stopped in front of Danny Hartmann. "What did she say when you asked her to explain?"

"Haven't asked her yet but I intend to today. I wanted to see if she'd said something to you that might help us understand what went on."

"No, she said she went to work at noon and home a little after nine. Other than that, all she said was that she's freaked. Thinks the same thing's happening that happened last year."

"I'm sorry, Sam."

"Don't be. You're not the one who lied to me . . . to us." He started to leave the office.

Danny rose from her chair. "Wait, I'm on my way to see Liz Fairchild." She turned to their boss. "Okay if Sam comes along? He's the one Liz agreed to see."

Angel nodded consent and the meeting broke up.

*

Sam and Danny drove separately to The Fairchild Gallery so his partner could go see Amanda afterwards. Since he wasn't exactly on a roll that morning, he was surprised when he scored a parking space right in front of the gallery.

He waited for Danny to join him, then knocked at the gallery door. Liz Fairchild immediately answered. Before he could finish introducing himself, Liz interrupted. "Of course I know who you are. I remember what you did last year for one of my best artists. Come in."

"This is Detective Danny Hartmann," Sam finished the introductions. "Thanks for seeing us before you open up."

"No problem. But I'm curious what the Portland Police Bureau thinks I can do to help them," Liz said as she led them through the gallery. It was elegant looking, all cream-colored walls, focused light and strategically placed partial walls at interesting angles. In the front of the gallery was an exhibit of scenes from the Southwest. In the back, the works of other artists were on the walls; metal sculpture and glass pieces were displayed on pedestals. In a simple but well-designed case, jewelry and smaller objects were arranged.

Her office, on the other hand, was decorated with nothing except a calendar and a large bulletin board covered in layers of announcements, postcards, and invitations. Which suited the furnishings—a battered desk and two equally beat-up file cabinets. Accommodations for visitors consisted of a couple of folding chairs. Only the computer looked state of the art. Liz clearly didn't waste money on anything her clients wouldn't see.

Sam and Danny opened the folding chairs and sat while Liz poured coffee for them, coffee that thankfully matched the classy gallery and not the office if the aroma was any indication. Settling in her desk chair with her mug, Liz looked from one detective to the other and said, "So, what can I do for you this morning?"

"Danny's the detective in charge of the Kane/Jordan case," Sam said. "We heard you had a run-in with Eubie Kane not long before he was killed. Mind telling us what it was about?"

She sniffed. "He's been a pain since I signed him for the gallery. His latest was trying to get out of his contract when he thought he could get into a gallery he considered a step up. I wouldn't let him go. I'd dropped a bundle for print ads announcing a solo show for him next month. That's what the run-in was about. He wanted out. I wouldn't let him, not without the two months' notice he agreed to. I was pissed at him, the little worm."

After she took a sip of her coffee, she continued. "Sorry. I'm not as insensitive as that sounds. Not even someone who was a pain in the ass should have his life cut short like that. And Robin Jordan. I heard she was a real sweetheart."

"Did you have trouble with him before the contract issue came up?" Danny asked.

"Oh, honey, all the time. He complained about everything." She imitated Eubie's whine. "The light's not right for my glass. Do something about it. Those pedestals don't show off my work to its best advantage. Get new ones." She threw up her hands and returned to her normal voice. "If he wasn't bitching about one thing, it was another."

"If he was that much trouble, why didn't you let him go?" Sam asked.

"Because I liked the work and it sold pretty well. I don't have to be an artist's best friend to represent them."

"Okay, so you and he had it out last Monday. You gave him a note?" Danny continued.

"He wouldn't listen when I said no, so finally I said maybe if I put it in writing he'd understand. I wrote, 'hell no, you can't go' or something like that on a piece of brown paper—I was hanging a show and the floor was littered with the stuff—and gave it to him. How'd you figure out I wrote it?"

"Part of a mailing label with your name on it was on the other side," Danny said.

"Remind me not to write any ransom notes, will you?" She got up from her desk and picked up the coffee carafe. Saying, "Let me freshen your coffee," she topped up the two visitors' mugs before emptying the remainder of the contents of the pot into her own.

"He got into it with Amanda St. Claire recently, accused her of stealing his ideas. Do you think there was any basis to that?" Sam asked.

"If anyone stole ideas, it was the other way around. Eubie was technically pretty good and people liked his work but he played it safe, did the same thing over and over. Not like Amanda who's always pushing herself and has an *omigod* originality that attracts critical attention."

"So, to have it for the record," Danny said, "Where were you Tuesday between say, seven and ten pm?"

"You mean this past Tuesday night?"

Danny nodded.

"Let's see—I had drinks with a friend. After that, I dropped by a new gallery that's trying to stay open late most nights. Wanted to see if they were getting any foot traffic. I went home after I had dinner. I was leaving for Seattle the next morning and wanted to get a good night's sleep."

"Where's home?" Danny asked.

"I live in the southwest, off Macadam Avenue."

"After you had drinks with your friend, were you with anyone who'll vouch for you?" Sam asked.

"No. Collins, my partner, isn't here right now."

Sam persisted. "You didn't stop anyplace else on your way home?"

Liz stood up and looked out into the gallery, as if she heard a noise.

Sam repeated the question.

"Drinks, dinner, home. That's about it." She sat down without looking directly at either detective.

"Anything else you think we should be aware of about Eubie Kane?" Danny asked. "Any enemies? Anybody who disliked him intensely enough to want to harm him?"

"Not that I can think of. He was always playing the tortured *artiste*, which was boring and annoying, but I can't think of anyone who truly hated him."

"So, who found him annoying?" Danny asked.

"Most recently? Me and another gallery owner, Sophie Woods. I talked to her right after he was here that Monday, and she was steaming about how much time she wasted talking to him when he knew he couldn't sign with her."

They asked a few more questions before winding up the interview, thanking Liz for her time. As they walked to Sam's truck, a young man with dark hair and a couple small Band-Aids on his face, as though he had cut himself shaving, walked past them, stopped close to the gallery and stared at them. Sam returned the stare until the man broke eye contact, knocked on the door of the gallery, and Liz let him in.

Danny stood by the driver-side door while Sam unlocked it. "She's not telling us everything," she said. "She skipped a step or two about what she did after she had drinks."

Sam nodded agreement. "And she must be six feet tall and left-handed from the way she picked up that coffee pot. She could have done what it would have been hard for Amanda to do. But would Robin Jordan have let her into Bullseye? And where's the motive? Would she kill the goose that laid the golden—or in this case, glass—egg? And fighting with Jordan that way? Killing her? I don't see it."

Danny didn't seem to be paying attention to Sam's musings. She was looking across the street. "That car over there. The guy working across the street from Bullseye that night not only saw Amanda's Highlander, he saw Eubie Kane's van, a beater Toyota Corolla, and what he called a classy looking silver or gray car, a BMW, he thought. That silver Beemer across the street from the gallery—wanna bet when I run the plate, it belongs to Liz?"

"She was there, too? Christ, what was going on at Bullseye, free beer night?"

"Liz strikes me as more the wine type but, other than that, I agree with you. After I see who owns that car I'll go back and ask her one more time where she was," Danny said, "before I go on to my next appointment."

"If you can let me know . . . " He didn't finish the sentence.

"I'll try, Sam. I promise."

*

Liz Fairchild let Mike Benson into the gallery and locked the door before she said, "You're not due to work today, Mike. And frankly I'm surprised you showed up at all. It's not often a thief returns to the place he robbed."

He handed her a fistful of bills. "I'm not a thief. I came by to give you the money for the bracelet. It was marked $95. It's all there. I shouldn't have taken it before I paid you but I had this hot date and wanted to give her a present. It was her birthday."

Liz took the money. "Why didn't you tell me? I would have let you take it and pay me later. You didn't have to steal it."

"I didn't steal it. You've been paid for it. You were on the phone when I left, remember? I didn't have a chance to ask you. And I had to get home to change."

"I guess I'll have to take your word for it," she said. Before she could say anything else, there was a knock on the door. Liz turned yelling, "We're not open until . . ." but stopped, mid-sentence, when she saw Danny Hartmann. "God, now what?" she muttered as she walked to open the door.

"What else can I do for you, Detective Hartmann?" Liz said when she let the officer back in. As the two women faced off in the middle of the gallery, Mike Benson disappeared out the front door. Neither woman paid attention.

"It's about your car over there," Hartmann said.

"It's legally parked, isn't it?"

"I don't do parking enforcement. I'm interested in whether you and your car were at Bullseye on Tuesday night."

"No, that's not the gallery I went to."

"I'm not talking about their gallery on Everett. I meant the Resource Center in the southeast."

"Why are you asking?"

"Around the time Eubie Kane and Robin Jordan were killed,

a man across the street from Bullseye saw a silver car parked out front that sounds a lot like yours."

"You think I killed them?"

"Not necessarily. But if you were there, you might have seen something that will help us figure out who did."

"I told you, I had drinks with a friend, went to a gallery over on the eastside, had dinner at Doug Fir, then I went home."

"You were at a gallery and a restaurant on the eastside, where Bullseye is? You didn't say that before. You were there—when? For how long?"

"It's not real clear. Maybe about seven, eight. For an hour or more, I'd guess."

"Which puts you driving home about nine. You could have been the Beemer owner who swung by Bullseye."

"I don't remember doing that. But then, I'd had several drinks."

"You sure that's the answer you want to give me?"

Liz didn't respond for a moment. "I'll call you if I remember anything else."

"You do that." Hartmann handed Liz a business card. "Here. For when your memory improves. I hope that happens soon." She was on the sidewalk before Liz could respond.

Chapter Ten

While Sam was doing all he could to figure out who had murdered two people, Amanda was paralyzed by anxiety. Her conscience told her she should tell Sam about the letters left when her studio was ransacked—but that was exactly what the note said would put Sam in danger. She couldn't have that. So, she ignored the voice and tried to work it out by herself.

In the end all she could do was a little office business and a bit of work on her propane torch. Moving stringers through the flame and watching drops of molten glass fall onto the table in perfectly rounded pieces was soothing. Or inhaling propane fumes was. She wasn't sure which and didn't really care, as long as it worked.

Then Felicia called and said the Resource Center had been cleared to reopen. Amanda shut off her torch, shook off her torpor, went to Bullseye and dropped a small fortune on sheet glass, hopeful that having supplies to get back to work with would get her out of her slump.

When Danny Hartmann arrived at her studio, she was unpacking and storing her precious cargo. They had an awkward conversation. Amanda tried to explain why she omitted—her word—her presence at Bullseye that night, saying she didn't think she'd seen anything worth reporting.

From the number of times and the variety of ways the question was asked about why she lied—Hartmann's word—Amanda knew Sam's partner didn't believe her. She tried to explain how frightened she was because of the similarities between what had happened last year and this latest horrible event, but she didn't think Hartmann was convinced.

Amanda didn't have the nerve to ask—or maybe didn't want to find out—if Sam knew she'd been there.

After Hartmann left, Amanda considered going home and hiding herself under the quilt on her bed. Instead, she buried herself in work, her lethargy gone with the need to clear her mind of what happened. She finished storing her purchases, cleaned out kilns, scraped shelves and painted them with kiln-wash so she could fire glass on them, and readied the bins of ruined work for trash pickup. It was long after dark when she finished her tasks, but for the first time in days she felt like she'd gotten real work done.

As soon as she had the last trashcan out on the sidewalk, she locked up the back door, shut off the lights in her work area, and walked toward the front of the studio. The only illumination came from the three glory holes. Normally she found the glow of the molten glass comforting. But tonight, something was off.

Mid-studio, she stopped and looked around, trying to figure it out. Everything looked normal. Nothing was out of place.

Wait. That sound. Was it wind against the metal building? No. There wasn't any wind. A neighbor putting out trash? The sound hadn't come from the direction of the street.

When it happened again, she recognized what it was—the metal door near her worktables being carefully rattled, as if someone were trying to see if it was open.

"Who's there?" she called.

There was no answer.

She tried again. "Who's at the back door?"

Still nothing.

Her cell phone rang. She jumped, then rummaged to find it at the bottom of her purse. It was Sam.

"Where are you?" he said. "I've been trying to find you."

"I'm just leaving the studio."

"You didn't answer when I knocked."

"Is that you at the back door? Why didn't you say so? You scared me when you didn't answer."

"It was a half hour ago, and I knocked at the front."

She heard the sound again. "Somebody's rattling the door. I better go."

"Someone's banging on your back door? Can you see who it is?"

"There aren't any windows in the back."

"And whoever it is didn't respond when you asked?"

"No."

"Where are you parked?"

"About four blocks away."

"That's too far. Don't hang up. I'll call for a patrol car. Wait for them, then go to your car and lock yourself in. Let the officers look around. Understand?"

"I can take care of calling the police."

"For chrissake, Amanda, just do as I say . . . "

She heard the sound of the phone receiver being dropped. Heard the low murmur of his voice as he spoke to the dispatcher on his cell phone. Heard the continued rattling of the back door. Standing in a deeply shadowed space between two kilns, she took a long, slow breath to calm her heart rate. Then she sidled toward the front door. She unlocked it, pulled her keys out of her purse, ready to run to her car when he got back on the phone. If he ever got back on the phone.

"Amanda?"

Finally. "What took you so long? You have me really scared," she whispered.

"A couple patrol cars are on the way. They won't run sirens but at least one of them will have lights flashing so you can identify them. I'll stay on the phone until you see them."

A crash, the sound of metal being smashed, came from the back of the studio. "I can't wait for them. The back door was just broken open."

"Get the hell out of there and run to your car."

She flung open the door and sprinted into the dark as fast as she could. She punched the remote for her car but in her panic, accidently pushed the emergency button. The lights on her Highlander flashed and the horn blew, raising her anxiety.

However, the officer in the patrol car who pulled up alongside her SUV a few seconds later told her how smart she was to identify her vehicle that way. Amanda didn't bother to correct the officer's impression of her intelligence. When she was safely inside the patrol car she got back on the phone with Sam.

"The patrol car's here, Sam. I'm with Officer . . . "

"Jefferson," the man said. "Officer Lopez is on his way. Is that Detective Richardson?" He put his hand out for the phone.

Amanda gave it to him. There wasn't much to hear from his end of the conversation other than the occasional, "uh-huh." When the conversation was finished, Jefferson handed the phone back to her. "How about we go see what's going on and lock up your studio? Lopez should be there. After we get that taken care of, one of us will follow you home. Detective Richardson will meet us there."

Back in the studio, they found a dented door and a broken lock. The office had been quickly searched, if the papers and boxes all over the floor and the open drawers and cabinets were any indication. Nothing in the studio itself was disturbed and nothing appeared to be missing.

With the officers' help, she jury-rigged the door shut. They barricaded the back with the desk and a worktable before locking up the front door. As requested, Officer Jefferson followed Amanda home where Sam was waiting.

After he talked to the officer, Sam joined Amanda inside. "Are you okay?" he asked.

"I've had better days." She motioned to him to take off his jacket.

He hesitated before removing it and handing it to her saying,

"Yeah, me, too." He looked weary, all of his thirty-six years evident in the lines in his face, which were deeper than usual. "Jefferson says nothing was missing. That true?"

"Sam, I . . . "

"Is that true?" he repeated.

She didn't answer for a bit, trying to read his expression. Finally she said, "Nothing seems to be missing, even the petty cashbox was intact. It may be time to move the studio—three break-ins in less than a month. That's some kind of record."

He didn't comment. She looked down at the floor, unable to face him. "Sam, I have to tell you something."

Turning away, he started for the door. "I know what you have to tell me, but I'm not sure I want to have this conversation tonight."

"You don't think I . . . ?" She couldn't even say the words.

"Killed Robin Jordan and Eubie Kane? Of course I don't. But you lied about being there. If you don't believe it's stupid to lie to the police, I'd have thought you trusted me enough not to lie to me."

The word "lie" hit her like a fist each time he said it. "I can explain. Please. Sit down for a minute. Just listen."

He followed her into the living room and sat facing her on the opposite couch, his face stony. "I'm listening."

"Of course I should have told you—told the police—I was there. But I felt trapped. Eubie Kane was on a rant about me. Leo's gun with my fingerprints on it killed him. I was only three blocks away. Motive, means, opportunity. It's like location, location, location." She looked up at him, but he didn't seem amused at her attempt to lighten the atmosphere.

"I couldn't say I'd been there. I knew what it looked like and I knew what you—what the police—would think. I would be presenting them with a neat little package that wrapped up their case. Just like last year. It was all back again. I couldn't be involved again, not when I hadn't done anything. So, I didn't tell anyone, figuring you'd find out who did it and I wouldn't have to. I should have known better but I was scared."

"Why were you there, Amanda?"

She moved a pillow from behind her and clutched it to her chest before she answered. "I'd agreed to meet him at my studio but I finished up earlier than I expected. I, uh, decided to go see him. He'd said he would be at Bullseye. I figured he was taking a class; that's the only reason anyone's there at night. And classes usually end by nine. I thought maybe I'd have a chance to snag him when it was over." Her voice trailed off.

"Okay, you went to see him. Go on."

"I got there and saw cars parked in the covered area near the front door so I thought my guess that he was in class was right. But when I got to the door, it was dark inside. No one answered when I knocked. I didn't expect it to be open. It never is when there's a class. But I banged hard enough that if someone was in there, they would have heard."

"The man who saw you says you went south on Twenty-first."

"Toward the factory, yeah. I knocked on the door to the office. No one answered. So I went around the block to see if I could find anyone. When I couldn't, I got in my car and came home."

"That took you ten minutes?"

"I have no idea how long it took me. I wasn't exactly timing myself."

"You didn't see anyone who can verify what you're saying?"

She broke eye contact with him and plucked at the corner of the pillow she was holding. "No one will verify it."

"Why'd you call Kane later?"

"To tell him I wouldn't be at the studio if he showed up."

"Why? You knew he wasn't at Bullseye like he said he'd be."

"I thought maybe he was in-between and I'd just missed him. It was raining so hard I could have driven right past him and not noticed. Anyway, I got no answer."

"And that's all?" He got up and walked over to her, tipped her chin up with his forefinger so she was looking at him. "Are you sure?"

She pulled her face away.

He watched her for a moment before rubbing his hand across his face. "It feels like you haven't told me the whole story. Like you don't trust me."

"I do trust Sam Richardson, the man I . . . the man I'm involved with. But I'm not sure I feel the same about Detective Richardson, the one who'd have to tell his partner what I said. But I swear to you, I didn't do anything wrong at Bullseye that night."

"Well, both Sam Richardson and Detective Richardson are happy to hear that, Amanda." He shook his head. "But, for future reference, it's a package deal. I can't be split in two." He went to the hall, grabbed his jacket, and went out the front door.

She sat on the couch, her head back, unable to move. When her phone indicated an incoming text message, it startled her. She pulled it from her pocket, looking to see if it was Sam apologizing for walking out.

It wasn't. She stared at the message, rereading it again and again. Chihuly jumped up on the couch beside her, licked her face and whined a little, demanding attention. Absentmindedly she gave him a pat or two. "I can't let anything happen to him, can I, boy? Not after what he's done for me." She stood up and walked her dog to the kitchen door. "I have what this guy wants. I'll just give it to him."

*

Sam pounded on the steering wheel of his truck as he waited for the light to change. He wasn't sure if he was angry or frustrated, or both. Every cop instinct he had said she wasn't telling him the truth. But he had no idea what she was lying about. Nor did he know where to start to find out.

When he got home, he tried calling her, to apologize for the way he left but he got voice mail. She wasn't picking up, apparently didn't want to talk to him. He left a message saying he was sorry and would apologize in person when they had dinner the following night.

But apologizing was only part of why he wanted to talk to her again. He wanted to get to the bottom of this. Fast. He had a bad feeling about this. A feeling she was in danger.

Chapter Eleven

By the next morning Amanda had a plan. Although she didn't know the name of the guy who'd contacted her, she now understood what he was after. He'd referred to it in the text he'd sent and it was obvious from what she found in her studio the morning after the murders. In the letter from Tom Webster, her late boyfriend had denied stealing money from his partners, saying Amanda had taken it from his apartment and he thought she'd hidden it in a "*safe*" place. That was what the intruders had been looking for in her house—a safe full of money.

She didn't know where the mythical safe was or how much this guy thought she'd stolen. But she could get money from her trust funds to bribe him. If he had the money, he'd leave her alone.

The anonymous text from the night before, like the anonymous note in her studio, also threatened Sam. So the second part of the plan was to keep him away from what she was doing, to keep him safe. She didn't know what would happen if Sam found out what she was doing. It could end any chance she had for a future with him but she didn't care. He had to be out of harm's way. And she was the only person who could make that happen.

She answered the text. Said she had what the sender demanded but it would take her a couple of days to get it. Then she'd deliver it someplace public. As long as he left them alone.

One more text and she'd head for her beach house where she'd be out of everyone's reach, even Sam's. Especially Sam's. She didn't know how much longer she could keep what she knew from him.

*

Sam picked up a message as he was walking up the steps into Central Precinct. It was from Amanda, canceling their dinner.

He went back down to the sidewalk, crossed the street to the park, and called her. He expected her to avoid answering but, surprisingly, she picked up.

"Amanda, I apologize for the way I left things last night. I'm sorry. I handled it badly."

"Did you get my text?

"A text message? Ah . . . what did it say?"

"I need to cancel tonight."

"I upset you. Let's talk."

"That's not it. I'm not feeling—I mean, I think maybe Chihuly's sick."

"Can I help you take him to the emergency vet clinic?"

"No, I just need to stay with him."

"I'll bring over take-out. You have to eat."

"He's not good with anyone other than me when he's feeling bad."

"Maybe we can have dinner tomorrow, after you see how he does. Will you call and tell me how things go?"

"Sure. I'll call."

"Amanda, I . . . " But he was talking to a dead phone.

He tried all weekend to get in touch with her. There was no response. When he drove by her house and her Highlander was gone, he went to the studio. She wasn't there, either, and Giles said he hadn't seen her.

Sam left notes, called, texted, emailed, patrolled her street looking for her. Nothing. Where the hell was she?

*

Monday morning, Amanda drove back from the coast and went directly to her bank. Her banker was concerned at the size of the withdrawal she wanted and politely asked what she was planning to do with it. A real estate deal, she said, with an eccentric old man who wanted cash. The banker knew she had a number of real estate investments so he reluctantly agreed. But it would take a couple days to get the cash.

*

Sam was waiting for the elevator when the door opened and Danny Hartmann got out, a paper cup in her hand. "Welcome to Monday," she said. "Have a good weekend?" She held the door for him.

He got on the elevator, seeming not to want to share what his weekend had been like. Finally he said, "It's over. That's the best I can say about it. How 'bout you?"

"Better than yours, from the tone of your voice." Sam let the elevator door close before she could say anything else.

She knocked on the door of Lt. Angel's office.

"Danny. Good. Come on in. Tell me what you have on Kane/Jordan."

"It gets curiouser and curiouser."

"Wouldn't have thought you were the Alice-in-Wonderland type, Danny. Although now that you mention it, you do resemble the Red Queen sometimes."

"Thanks for the compliment. If that's a compliment, which I don't think it is. And how the hell do you know about Alice in Wonderland?"

"Five daughters, remember? Ask me anything about Disney princesses, Alice, Hermione. I've read it all." He sighed. "Not one super hero or G.I. Joe."

"At least with Hermione you got Harry Potter."

"Yeah, a fucking wizard. But that's not what you have for me, is it?"

Danny set her coffee cup on his desk and summarized what Amanda had told her. "She may have been wrong to withhold telling us she was there but she's right about one thing—there are too many similarities to the Webster case for coincidence. And all those coincidences wrap it up neatly. Also like last year."

She finished off her coffee and pitched the cup in the trashcan. "We're being led by our noses to see Amanda St. Claire as the perp. Why the similarities to the Webster case, I haven't figured out yet, but I will."

"She has a motive."

"Weak, according to the folks I've talked to but, interestingly, established publicly in front of half the Bullseye staff."

"You think one of them is our perp?"

"I think Kane wanted an audience to establish she had a reason to hate him. I don't like the time element either. The guy across the street says she was there less than ten minutes. I don't think she could have done what was done in ten minutes. Add a left-handed perp who brought down a six-footer and the image it paints for me isn't Amanda St. Claire."

"Okay, for the moment, let's accept what you say is true," Lt. Angel said. "That still leaves her lying about being there. Why?"

"I think she saw something and is too scared to tell me. Maybe the murderer or someone she knew. I'm not sure. I wish she'd trust me enough to talk to me honestly."

"Let me think about this for a while. Got anything else?"

"A few odds and ends. The guy who saw Amanda there also saw a 'classy car,' as he described it. Silver, he thought, or gray, probably a BMW. Liz Fairchild, who owns the gallery where Kane showed his work, has a silver BMW and was on the eastside that night. She was evasive about where she was, even intimated that she might have been a little drunk. I think she was at Bullseye, too."

"Could Amanda have seen her? Maybe that's who she's trying to protect. I imagine they're acquainted."

"Yeah, they are. The Fairchild Gallery represents Amanda. Maybe they're each protecting the other."

Lt. Angel got up from his desk. "I'd congratulate you on your work but since you're right, it's Wonderland quality, I'll save the awards and decorations until you come back with a name. I will say you've turned over a lot of interesting rocks. What's next?"

"I want to find out whose fingerprints are on the kiln controller and the glass, so I'll nag the lab. And I'm going back to the Pearl to talk to Liz Fairchild. Maybe now that she's had a chance to think things over, she'll have more to say to me."

*

"Detective Hartmann, how nice to see you again." Liz Fairchild greeted the police officer as she opened the door. "But I'd appreciate it if you'd come during regular gallery hours to see what my artists are exhibiting."

"Sorry to inconvenience you, Ms. Fairchild, but this isn't so much about art appreciation as an appreciation for the truth. Or lack of it, in this case."

"Oh, my, you're more confrontational than you were the last time you were here."

"That was the good cop. I'm here today as the bad cop."

"I thought that was a game you played with two officers."

"We're understaffed. Can we go back to your office for a few minutes?"

Liz led the way. "Okay," she said when they were both seated, "what now?"

"Unless you want to spend the afternoon at the precinct with your lawyer and a couple of officers really playing good-cop/bad-cop, you can tell me the truth about what you saw at Bullseye when you were there the night of the murder."

Liz took a deep breath and rummaged around aimlessly on

the top of her desk. Eventually she looked straight at Danny Hartmann.

"Look, I didn't lie. I just left out a few things."

"Lot of that going around," Danny said.

"I got a phone call while I was eating dinner. A voice whispered that if I wanted to get the contract thing straightened out with Eubie, I should get to Bullseye ASAP."

"Did you recognize the voice?"

"No. But I went anyway. It wasn't much of a detour to swing by Bullseye on my way home so I thought what the hell, I might as well go see what he had to say."

"What did you see while you were there?"

"The building was dark. No signs anyone was there, except for what was parked in the covered parking area: an old brown hatchback, Eubie's van, and . . . and a red SUV. Amanda St. Claire's. With her vanity plate, it's easy to identify."

"Was she in her vehicle?"

"No, I didn't see a living soul. Or a dead one."

"So, what did you do?"

"It was pouring rain so I stayed in the car and waited for a couple minutes to see if anyone came out. No one showed so I left."

"Any idea what time it was?"

"Around nine, I'd guess."

"You're sure that's all."

"Yes, Detective Hartmann. That's all. I didn't kill anybody. I didn't see anyone get killed."

"But you saw Amanda St. Claire's SUV there about the time two people were killed and that's why you've been evading my questions."

Liz sighed. "Yes, I did and that's why I have been."

Chapter Twelve

Guilt—actually fear of getting caught—had kept Sam from any more snooping around his partner's desk. But the next morning, delivering a cappuccino he'd gotten for her when he got his morning latte, he saw a report on fingerprints he couldn't resist checking out.

What it said sent him back to his computer for a quick search of the old Webster case records.

And there it was: the fingerprints found on the glass from the big kiln at Bullseye belonged to Beal Matthews, a low-level thug hired by Tom Webster to run errands for the drug ring. He'd been dimed out by the cops who'd been involved in the operation, had served time for possession and been released about two months prior because of good behavior and jail overcrowding.

But it was Matthews booking photo that made him mutter, "I'll be damned." Staring back at him from his computer screen was the man he seen entering The Fairchild Gallery the day he and his partner interviewed Liz.

As the printer chugged out a copy of the photo, he called Matthews' parole officer. The p.o. said Matthews had been a model prisoner and had been following all the rules since he'd been out. Sam got a home and work address as well as the information that Matthews had recently been doing some part-time work for a business in the Pearl, but the p.o. didn't know where. Sam did.

He grabbed the copy of the booking photo and his coffee and headed out to his pickup before anyone—read, L.T.—could stop him or ask what he was working on.

At the car repair shop where Matthews worked, the owner said his employee had called in sick that morning, a first. Matthews wasn't at his apartment, either. An apartment Sam wasn't surprised to see was close to both Amanda's studio and Bullseye.

He debated stopping by the GlassCo studio but decided not to. Amanda still hadn't returned his calls and he wasn't sure he wanted to find out what that meant just yet. Deal with one crisis at a time was his motto for the day.

Instead, he checked Eubie Kane's neighborhood. Kane's next-door neighbor thought Matthews might have been hanging out with Kane for the month or two before he was killed. The neighbor wasn't positive. Kane's new friend seemed shy, didn't like to talk, always wore a hoodie with his face obscured or a baseball cap pulled down on his forehead.

Last, he went to The Fairchild Gallery where Liz confirmed that Beal Matthews was Mike Benson. She also told Sam about the gold bracelet he'd taken from her gallery to give to his hot new girlfriend for her birthday.

He hadn't found his suspect but at least he could confirm for the parole officer where his client had been working part-time. And the mysteries of Robin Jordan's gold bracelet and her secret boyfriend seemed to have been solved.

Sam drove back downtown to Central Precinct sure in his belief that Beal Matthews was the man they were looking for. All they had to do was find him.

*

Danny Hartmann couldn't decide if she was pissed, scared or frustrated. Acting on the fingerprint information on her desk, she'd begun the legwork to track down Beal Matthews. Only to find out that every phone call, every visit was on the heels of one from Sam. She was pissed at his going off on his own, scared he'd get caught and suffer the consequences, frustrated that he didn't trust her enough to take her into his confidence.

She almost blew off a visit to Amanda's studio assuming Sam had gone there, too. But when she thought about it, he'd been adamant that Amanda had been out of contact so she took a chance and went to the GlassCo studio to see if Amanda recognized Beal Matthews. Only Leo Wilson was there. He identified the man in the photo as Mike, a guy who lived in the neighborhood and who'd dropped by a few times to talk about blowing glass.

She also learned "Mike" had asked a lot of questions about how they protected themselves from robbery when the area was deserted at night and Leo had told him about the gun they kept in the office. He couldn't say for sure "Mike" knew where it was but it was possible he'd seen it when Leo had opened the drawer for a pen and paper to write down a phone number.

That left only one place to go—Amanda's house.

"This isn't a good time, Detective Hartmann," Amanda said when she opened the door.

"It'll only take a minute." Hartmann pulled Matthews' picture out of her leather bag. "Have you ever seen this guy?"

Danny watched Amanda's expression harden. "I said, I can't talk to you right now. Please go."

"This is important. Leo says this guy dropped by the studio on several occasions. Maybe you saw his car? We think it's an old Toyota hatchback."

Shock broke through her neutral expression but Amanda still didn't say anything.

Danny waited a few moments to see if there was more. "Nothing rings a bell?"

Amanda just stared at her.

"Couple other things might interest you: he's been living about two blocks away from your studio and Bullseye." She paused. "Oh, and he worked for Tom Webster selling drugs. Got out of prison a couple months back."

The look of steely determination returned. "I have to go,

Detective Hartmann." Amanda started to close the door.

Danny put a foot on the threshold to keep the door from shutting. "We think he killed Eubie Kane and Robin Jordan. I also think he set out to mimic the circumstances of the Webster murder. Any idea why he'd want to do something like that?"

Amanda looked straight into Danny's eyes. "Do you know how hard it was to get past the hell I went through last year because of what Tommy and a couple of your less-than-honorable colleagues did? I had to leave town to get away from the gossip even after the court acknowledged I wasn't guilty of anything other than bad judgment in my personal life."

"I appreciate what happened to you, Amanda."

"I doubt that, Detective Hartmann. Portland can be a small town and it's easy to have your reputation wrecked by careless police work and bad press coverage. I hope you never find out how easy."

She pushed the door against Hartmann's foot. "So, in case I haven't been clear, listen up. I had nothing to do with what Tommy did; I had nothing to do with what happened at Bullseye. Other than that, I have nothing to say to you. And if you want to talk to me again, I need advance notice so I can have my lawyer with me."

Hartmann removed her foot from the doorway. Amanda slammed the door.

*

"Hartmann. My office. Now." L.T. bellowed from the door of his office. Everyone within earshot turned to see what was going on. No one could remember hearing Chris Angel yell like that before.

Sam looked up from his computer at his partner. She shrugged her shoulders as if to say, "I have no idea," and did as she had been commanded. Sam went back to what he'd been working on, afraid there would be another shoe dropped soon.

Less than five minutes later at an identical decibel level, Angel yelled, "Richardson. Now you."

Angel closed the door behind him and waved Sam to a chair. Danny was sitting in another chair, looking subdued, the remains of a blush on her cheeks. He'd never seen her look so deflated.

"I got three phone calls this morning from a parole officer and two citizens asking why we were so disorganized that there were multiple visits within an hour from police officers asking the same questions. You know anything about that, Detective Richardson?"

"I don't think so."

"The hell you don't. You were one of the officers asking questions about Kane/Jordan. After I directly told you to keep out of the case."

"Multiple? Who . . . ?" He looked at his partner who nodded her head.

"Yeah, she was the other one. But she didn't bother to tell me what you were up to. Did you ask her not to?" the lieutenant asked.

"I didn't tell her anything. I wasn't going to risk her career."

"Just yours."

"Which is mine to risk. I couldn't sit around and do nothing."

"You disobeyed a direct order. You mucked around with witnesses. You could have made them useless in a prosecution. You put your partner in an untenable situation." Angel blew out a breath. "What the fuck should I do with you?"

"Put me on administrative leave," Sam said.

"So you can have an even freer rein to mess around in this case? Like hell I will. I was leaning more toward protective custody."

Sam did a double take. "I didn't do anything illegal."

"The hell of it is, I'm at the place where I need you to be involved in this case. If you'd waited one more day . . . "

"What do you want me to do?" Sam asked.

"I'm not sure I trust you to do what I ask."

127

"I apologize. I thought I was onto something. I should have kept you in the loop. Now, please, let me help." He hoped he sounded sincere. Because he was, about one thing—he sincerely believed he'd do anything to get back on this case.

Angel stared long enough at Sam to make him uncomfortable. "What the fuck? I don't really have much of a choice. Okay, Danny, tell him what you told me earlier."

Danny said, "I was at Amanda's house this morning. She wouldn't let me in but we talked at the door. About two minutes into the conversation, something I said triggered a look on her face, like she was remembering something. Then the interview went off the cliff. She asked me to leave and not come back without an appointment so she could have her attorney with her."

Angel said, "I was planning on asking you to see if she'd talk to you, Sam, before I found out what you'd been up to. Now . . . "

"L. T., I know you're not happy with either of us," Danny began. "But you need to let Sam talk to her. I think she saw Matthews there that night. And he's the only one who can find out if she did."

"If she ID's him, that puts her in danger until we have him in custody. You have his prints on the kiln and on that glass. Why do you need her?" Sam asked.

Angel hesitated, as if still not sure he should be letting Sam back in. Finally he said, "There are too many holes in the case." He ticked them off. "No motive. The only good ID we have is Leo Wilson's and that puts Matthews in the neighborhood along with anyone who works in the Fred Meyer corporate headquarters and the other neighbors. We can't ID the Toyota as his. No car is registered in his name." Angel came out from behind his desk and perched on the edge of it in front of Sam as he continued.

"He could tell us he left the prints on Kane's glass and at Bullseye some other time and we couldn't dispute it. If Amanda St. Claire can place him there at the right time that night, can connect the dots about the car, we're on more solid ground."

"Okay, okay, I get it." Sam looked up at the ceiling, closed his eyes, shook his head, then looked at his boss. "This isn't how I wanted back in, L.T."

"It's the best you're gonna get from me at the moment. I need her cooperation. I have to use you."

"Not sure she'll even talk to me."

"Nice to know you're not any happier about this than I am. But I want this case wrapped up ASAP. Go do it."

*

When the doorbell rang, Amanda was sure Danny Hartmann had returned and she answered, ready to give the cop a tongue-lashing.

But instead of the police detective, standing on her doorstep was the man in the photo Danny had shown her. The man who had stalked her while she shopped.

The man she'd seen at Bullseye the night two people were murdered.

She cleared her throat, sure her voice would wobble when she spoke. Finally she said, "Yes, can I help you? Are you lost?"

"No, Amanda. I'm exactly where I want to be." Beal Matthews pushed past her into the hallway. "Now, we're going to go open that safe and get out what you owe me."

"What safe? There's no safe," she said. She realized her mistake when she saw the furious look on his face. "That is, there's nothing in the safe. It all went into my bank account. I told you. My banker will be getting the money tomorrow."

"Bitch." He slapped her across the face. "You're lying. You stole from Tom, you killed him and got away with it, you're still trying to cheat me. Show me where the damn safe is or that's just a taste of what you're in for." Twisting her arm behind her, he shoved her toward the kitchen. "We're going downstairs. That's where it has to be. But I can't find it. Move. Now." He pulled a gun from his pocket. "Or I'll use this."

Chihuly appeared from the kitchen, growling at Matthews, teeth bared.

"Goddamn dog." He pointed the gun at Chihuly's head. "Get rid of him."

Amanda tried to move in front of her dog. "Don't hurt him."

"You're right. He didn't cheat me out of what I earned. But if you don't get rid of him, he'll pay for what you did."

"Okay, okay, I'll put him out if you'll let me go." Followed by Matthews, Amanda led her dog by the collar to the back door and pushed him outside.

"Now, you, downstairs," Matthews stuck the muzzle of the gun in her ribs.

She opened the door, flipped on the light at the top of the steps and descended, followed by Matthews. When she got to the bottom, she indicated the drifts of packing paper, empty storage boxes and other detritus on the floor and said, "I gather you've been here before. But knock yourself out."

"You know where it is. Just show me." He motioned her toward the rabbit warren of rooms beyond.

Amanda didn't know what to do next. She had no idea if there was anything like a safe there, much less where it was. The police had looked. Sam had looked. Apparently Matthews had looked, too. No one had found anything.

She glanced around, wondering where to send him. She stored cobwebs, dust, and things she couldn't bear to part with in the various small rooms but none of them had doors behind which to trap him nor was there anything she could see to use to disarm him.

"I can't really remember where it is," she began. "It was a long time ago when Tommy told me about it."

He raised his hand to slap her again. She winced and his laugh was cocky-sounding, as if sure of his power over her. "You're too young to have that bad a memory. Tell me or I'll use this in a way you won't like." He leveled the gun at her. "Your boyfriend won't be so crazy about you if that pretty face is all messed up."

She put her hand up as if to ward off whatever he had in mind, then pointed toward the front of the house. "Wait, now I remember, it was behind the furnace." It was all she could think of. Maybe while he was back there, she could find a weapon, get out the back door. Something.

"There?" he said, gesturing toward the front wall.

She nodded.

"Move over here where I can see you while I look."

Amanda did as he ordered. As soon as he had squeezed behind the furnace and was occupied inspecting the wallboard, she looked around again for something to use as a weapon. The only thing that looked likely was a rake propped against the wall with other garden tools. She began to edge her way toward it.

Then, through the small window at ground level in the front of the house, she saw a black Mercedes pull up at the curb. Drake Vos got out and began to walk up the path to her front door. The relief that washed over her was so overwhelming her knees almost buckled. If she could get upstairs, Drake would help her keep Matthews there until they called the police.

When Matthews was completely behind the furnace, she made a run for the steps. Once upstairs in the kitchen, she locked the door to the basement and ran to open the front door.

"Drake, thank God. I've got the man who killed Eubie Kane and Robin Jordan in the basement. We have to call the police. Do you have a phone?"

Drake pulled a gun from his jacket pocket. "This will be more useful, I think."

"Yes, that'll help keep him here until they get here. But we have to call nine-one-one. I'll go get my . . . "

"No, Amanda. You won't." He took her arm. "I wouldn't want the police interrupting the job that Mr. Matthews and I have to take care of. Now, how about we join my colleague downstairs and finish this up."

Chapter Thirteen

Amanda stared at the second handgun pointed at her that day. "I don't believe this. You're involved, too?"

"Sorry to disappoint you, my dear, but involved I am. Now, down we go and let's get this settled. Matthews tells me you can show us where the safe is."

"Matthews is wrong."

"But you told him . . . "

"I told him I'd give him what he wanted, which I thought was money. I arranged to take money out of my trust fund accounts to bribe him to leave me and Sam alone."

"The man is an idiot." He waved her toward the kitchen. "However, that doesn't change the fact that Webster put a safe someplace. In the restaurant I found a combination that doesn't work anything there and Matthews had that letter. We've been through your studio, the restaurant, and most of your house. The basement is the most likely place. So, if you will accompany me . . . "

He motioned her to the door and, once again, reluctantly, she descended to the basement. When Matthews saw them, the anger on his face turned to a sneer.

"So much for trying to outthink us, bitch. Now get over here and show me where the fucking safe is."

"She doesn't know where it is," Vos said.

"Of course she does. She took the money and put it in her account. She told me."

"You fool," Vos said. "She's using money from her trust accounts to bribe you. We still don't know where the safe is."

Matthews slapped Amanda. "You little bitch." He raised his hand to hit her again.

Vos intervened. "Enough. We're going to be civilized about this. Amanda, sit on that chair over there. Matthews, watch her. I'm going to finish looking down here."

"She said she thought it was behind the furnace. I started back there but then she ran."

Vos looked at Amanda, now seated on an old plastic garden chair. "If you don't know where it is, Amanda, why did you tell him that?"

"I thought he'd be trapped back there and I could go get help."

Gesturing to the clutter around them, Vos said, "It's obvious most of the place has been searched. Did anyone look behind the furnace?"

Silence gave him the answer.

"All right, then I'll start there. If I come up empty, we can all resume the search elsewhere." He squeezed behind the furnace and began to rap on the wallboard. As he continued along the wall, he seemed to get more interested. He'd apparently seen or heard something Amanda couldn't figure out from where she was sitting.

But as he moved back and forth from one panel to another, comparing sounds, inspecting the surfaces, Amanda began to hear the difference between most of the panels of drywall and one particular panel, a panel that wasn't as dingy as the rest.

"Your instincts were good after all, Amanda. I need a hammer." Vos said. He nodded to Matthews to let her find one for him.

She dug her toolbox out of the mess on the floor, found a hammer, and handed it to him. He began to rip at the panel of odd-looking wallboard.

"I don't believe it," Amanda said when she saw the safe mounted between the studs he uncovered. She was sure the shock she felt showed on her face.

"Unless you are a considerably better actor than I think you are, I would say it's a surprise to you," Vos said. Glancing at a piece of paper he dug from his pocket, he began to dial in the combination. When the door of the safe opened, he grabbed a plastic bag from inside and tossed it to the floor. Bundles of bills tumbled out.

"That's it," Matthews said, his eyes bright with greed.

"That's only part of it." Digging further back Vos brought out a second bag. He looked in and smiled. "Ah, here's what I was looking for."

"Not money?" Amanda asked.

"No, Webster was not only stealing money from us but skimming drugs, too." A third bag came out, and a fourth. "Until Mr. Matthews showed me that letter, I thought the cops had found it all. But here it is and it's all ours." Vos reached into the back of the safe, checking to make sure he had everything. "That should do it. We're out of here, Beal."

*

Sam had started looking for Amanda at her studio but she wasn't there. Before heading for her house, he stopped at a Starbucks to brood over a cup of coffee. He really didn't like this assignment. Tracking her down to her house was probably the worst thing he could do. Something was wrong and he didn't know what. All he knew was it related to the two murders. But he didn't know how. He knew she was no more guilty of murdering two people than he was. He also knew she was hiding something. Lying to him.

If he had any chance of getting them back to where they were before this all blew up, it depended on finding out what the fuck was going on. He figured he had a fifty-fifty chance of getting her to talk to him so he could figure it out. Same odds for pissing her off so badly, she'd never see him again. He gulped down the remains of his lukewarm coffee and headed out to see which way luck was breaking for him.

When he arrived at her house he was relieved to see her SUV in the driveway. Until he saw what was parked next to it—an old brown Toyota hatchback like the car they thought Beal Matthews drove. And parked at the curb in front was a black Mercedes. Drake Vos's car, if he remembered right. What the hell was going on? Both Vos and the killer inside with Amanda?

He parked down the hill, out of sight of the house, and after calling for backup walked up to her side yard gate. Quietly, gun drawn, he went round to the back, hoping he could get the door to the basement open without any problem. He'd wait in the basement until backup arrived.

But as soon as he turned the corner into the yard, he was met with a bigger problem—Chihuly, so happy to see his friend, he barked and barked and barked to let Sam know he was ready to play.

*

Amanda heard the noise. "Something's wrong. Chihuly never barks like that."

"The hell with the dog," Matthews said. "We're out of here."

Chihuly kept barking, coming closer to the door to the basement.

"Matthews, go outside and see what's going on," Vos said. "We can't afford to get the neighbors curious. One of them already recognized me when I got out of my car."

Reluctantly, Matthews went to the back door. Amanda's dog was standing on the other side of the wall of rhododendrons, apparently intimidated by the thorns on the wildly growing rose bushes. The object of his attention hadn't been afraid of the thorns but his gun hand had gotten caught on a rose cane when he worked his way behind the bushes. Matthews took advantage of Sam's predicament, chopped at his hand to disarm him and,

136

ripping him free of the thorns, dragged him into the basement.

"Look who was lurking in the yard, Drake," he said.

"Detective Richardson. To what do we owe this honor?" Vos said.

"Amanda, are you all right?" Sam asked, walking to her and circling her shoulders with an arm.

"I'm okay," she answered. "Did he hurt you?"

"Aww. This is so touching," Matthews said. He pulled Amanda away from Sam by grabbing her hair and twisting it. Hard. She yelped. Matthews did it again, seeming to enjoy the pain he was causing. Sam took a swipe at him, connecting with his shoulder but without enough force him drop him.

Regaining his balance, Matthews hit Sam across the face with the gun. "Touch me again, cop, and you're dead."

"Touch her again and you'll be singing soprano for your new friends in the pen. I imagine some of them will like that," Sam responded.

Vos stepped between the two men. "That's enough. Focus on what's important, Matthews—getting out of here." He grabbed Sam's arm and pushed him onto another plastic chair.

"Which one are we going to take with us?" Matthews asked, waving the gun at Sam and Amanda. "We need insurance."

"No hostages," Vos said. "It looks too suspicious leaving the house that way." Before Matthews could object he said, "We take them upstairs, restrain them some way and then we leave one at a time. You take the money; I'll take the other bags. We meet at the rendezvous spot in an hour and then take off from there."

It was apparent that Matthews didn't agree but he gave in reluctantly, handed the bag with the money in it to Amanda, stuck his gun in her back and pushed her up the stairs. Vos followed with Sam carrying the bags of drugs, Vos's gun against his side.

When they got to the kitchen, Vos rummaged through drawers looking for something to use to restrain the two hostages. He found a plastic tie with which he secured one of Amanda's arms to a bar stool while he kept looking. Finally he found a small roll of duct tape.

"Here," he said to Matthews. "This will do for a start. Get Richardson taped to a chair and then look for something more secure for Amanda. I'll leave now; you get them tied up and leave in fifteen minutes."

"What's the damn hurry?" Matthews said. "Help me with this." He had pulled out a length of duct tape but was having trouble keeping it from sticking to itself.

"The hurry is the business I have to take care of before we leave. Take care of this yourself."

"Why the fuck didn't you take care of it before you came here?" Matthews asked.

"You dragged me away from home saying it was an emergency. So you get what you get. Shut up and take care of them." And he left.

When Amanda heard the door slam behind Vos, she shivered. He may have been a bad guy but he had some regard for her. Matthews was another matter. She was sure both she and Sam were in more danger now than they'd been a minute ago. Who knew what his idea of taking care of them would be?

As if to confirm her fears, Matthews grabbed her around the neck and pulled her against him. "So, cop, I have your girlfriend. You want her in one piece, find me some more tape or some rope."

"Leave her out of this, Matthews. She can't go anyplace tied to that bar stool. Just deal with me and I'll keep her from doing anything foolish."

"Yeah, you're a real white hat, aren't you? Do as I tell you or you'll be the reason she gets hurt."

Sam took a step toward Matthews who tightened his hold on Amanda's throat. Sam backed off, the expression on his face anguished. "Amanda, I . . . "

Amanda coughed to clear her airway before saying, "There's more duct tape over there, Sam. Where the string is." She hitched her chin toward the cabinet, hoping he remembered the evening he'd gone looking for string so she could tie up a roast. In the same cabinet he'd discovered miscellaneous strange travel souvenirs from her brother including a big, nasty Indonesian tribal knife and an Alaskan Ulu knife. Matthews started to follow Sam to the cabinet, giving Amanda the chance she wanted. She slid off the bar stool and took steps toward the back door, dragging the heavy seat with her.

"Don't move, bitch. I want you where I can see you," Matthews pointed the gun first at Sam, then at Amanda, seeming to be nervous about watching both of them.

"Chihuly's barking again. I want to let him in. If I don't he'll be scratching at the door."

"Leave it. I don't want a dog in here."

"But he'll annoy the neighbors. And damage the door."

"I said, leave it."

"I can't. I have to let the dog in."

As Amanda had hoped, the argument she'd incited forced Matthews to pay more attention to her than to what Sam was doing. She saw him palm the Ulu knife under the role of duct tape and approach Beal Matthews from behind.

But he didn't get to him fast enough. Matthews turned to see what he was doing before Sam could reach him. He might not have seen the Ulu knife but he surely saw the look on Sam's face, which was anything but compliant. He raised the gun, aiming directly at him.

Dropping the tape, Sam lunged at Matthews, catching his arm with the sharp blade of the knife. Matthews swore, knocked the weapon out of Sam's hand and grabbed for him. As the two men wrestled for control of the gun, Amanda picked up the knife, cut the plastic tie, opened the door and let Chihuly in. He joined the melee in the kitchen, barking and nipping at Matthews.

Amanda ran to the dining room for her phone. But before she could call nine-one-one, the sound of two gunshots came from the kitchen, followed by a loud thud and Chihuly yelping. Before she could yell for Sam, Matthews appeared in the doorway, bleeding from his arm and hands. He held the gun with a shaky grip.

"You bitch. I got shot because of you." He raised the gun, but before he could pull the trigger, Chihuly came from behind him and chomped on his hand. Matthews tried to shake off the dog. Amanda picked up the nearest thing heavy enough to do damage. She took two steps toward Matthews, swung and hit him right above the ear. The large glass plate she'd used broke; he crumbled. Cracking his head on the edge of the dining room table he fell to the floor, unconscious. Chihuly whimpered.

She saw blood on his fur, realized that Matthews might not have been the only one shot. And she hadn't heard Sam. "Oh, my God. Sam? Are you okay?"

There was no answer. She ran to the kitchen. Sam was on the floor, bleeding from his left shoulder, his right arm at an odd angle. "Sam! Are you . . . ?"

He got out, "Use that duct tape on Matthews. Danny . . . out front," before he passed out.

Chapter Fourteen

Amanda couldn't believe what a rapid and massive response an "officer down" call triggered. Within minutes of Danny's call, the first patrol car was there, then an ambulance for Sam, more patrol cars and another ambulance. Danny had waylaid Drake Vos outside Amanda's house as he left, handing him over to one of the uniformed officers before taking charge of getting the crime scene organized. Beal Matthews was loaded into the second ambulance.

Happy to leave a familiar face to deal with her house, Amanda started out the door to follow the ambulance taking Sam to the ER. Danny took the car keys from her hand and put them on the dining room table. "Talk first. Hospital later. You shouldn't drive right now and they won't let you see Sam anyway. What the hell happened here?"

Amanda took a deep breath and let out a barrage of words. "Beal Matthews came here to get the money from the safe Tommy put in my basement. Drake Vos came to help. After Drake found the safe, Chihuly barked and Matthews found Sam in the backyard. Sam cut Matthews with an Ulu knife. Sam got shot while I was looking for my phone. Matthews came to shoot me. Chihuly bit him. I hit Matthews with my glass . . . "

"Sorry I asked. Let's go over that again. Why did you say Matthews was here?"

Amanda dropped her eyes and made little coughing noises before answering. "Because I told him I knew where the safe was. That I'd give him money. I thought I could get him off my back, keep him away from Sam, if I paid him off. Then you would find him, arrest him, and everything would be okay."

"How the hell did you even know who he was? Unless . . . you did recognize him when I showed you his picture, didn't you?"

Another deep breath before the last confession came out in a whisper. "Yeah, I saw him at Bullseye the night of the murders. He threatened me and Sam if I talked to you. I knew he thought there was money here from Tommy's drug business so when I got a second threat from him, I decided to bribe him." She ran out of explanation and stopped talking, still not looking Danny in the eyes.

Danny exploded. "What the fuck is wrong with you, woman? How many times have we talked—three, four times? And you didn't tell me any of this? What kind of game are you playing?"

"I'm not playing a game. I was scared he'd hurt Sam. Besides, it didn't seem important." She knew she sounded as feeble as her excuse did.

"You don't get to decide what's important and what's not. We do. You tell us everything you know, we put it together with what we know and we figure out what happened. That's how it works."

"Not always."

"I got the message. You had a bad experience last year. Props to you for getting through it." Danny paced in front of Amanda, who was now sitting on the couch. "But that doesn't give you a pass on this. What were you waiting for, another person to turn up dead?"

Amanda shuddered. "That's exactly what I didn't want. I'm sorry, Danny, I should have . . . "

"Bullshit."

Amanda hung her head for a moment then looked directly at Danny. "I was stupid. If I'd been thinking clearly I wouldn't have even been at Bullseye that night. But the phone call I got said Eubie was about to go public with his accusations. I went to meet him. That's when I saw Matthews. He came out into the delivery area, outside the classroom. I could see him in the security light."

She rummaged around in her pocket, found a tissue, and blew her nose. "The next morning, I found the studio wrecked and an envelope with letters in it. From him. I have them here. I can get them . . . "

Danny didn't seem to be listening. "You lied about being at Bullseye. When we caught you at it, you still didn't tell us the whole story. You lied about what you saw there. Then you tried to bribe a killer to . . . " She stopped. "Wait. Rewind. You decided to bribe him because he threatened Sam?" She stared at Amanda. "Oh, shit, you pushed Sam away because you thought that would protect him, didn't you? I can't believe it."

Amanda closed her eyes. "Last year, because of me, he was suspended for months. He could have lost his whole career. And it was happening again. Only this time it was more than his career, it was his life. I wasn't going to put him in danger. Not after everything he'd done for me." She opened her eyes. Danny was staring at her in disbelief.

"Did you tell him?" Danny shook her head. "What am I saying? Of course you didn't. Jesus, did you really think you could bribe Matthews?"

"I thought all he wanted was money. And I had money. It's never been an issue with me."

"Aren't you lucky?"

"Yeah, I am. I've always had some measure of security because I had a trust income to fall back on. This time having it didn't help me." She looked up at Danny. "Are we finished here? Can I go now?"

"No, we're not finished. I have a feeling we won't be finished for days. But we can go to the hospital. I'll drive and we'll talk more on the way."

*

When they got to the hospital, Sam was in surgery. The ER nurse directed them to a waiting room where, she said, the doctor would come out when the surgery was over. Margo Keyes and Lt. Angel were already there, standing in a corner talking quietly.

"What are you doing here, Margo?" Amanda asked.

"Someone from the DA's office always comes out to something like this. I was up in the rotation," she said.

"Do you know how Sam is?"

Lt. Angel answered Amanda's question. "ER doc said he had an entry wound in the front of his shoulder, no exit wound. Broken arm. Fair amount of bleeding. They have him in surgery now getting the bullet out, the bleeders tied off, and his arm taken care of. He was semi-conscious when they admitted him."

"What about Matthews?" Danny asked.

"Bullet grazed his arm. He had cuts on his hands and arms and a dog bite. He was treated and released into custody. Oh, and he has quite a goose egg on his head. I understand he has you to thank for that, Ms. St. Claire. Nice hit. We'll be watching him for a concussion in the jail."

"And Drake Vos?" Amanda asked, ignoring the compliment.

"He's not talking much. But I think he will. What little he's said is to distance himself from the murders. He says Matthews was convinced you'd killed Tom Webster and he was trying to get his revenge for your 'getting away with it' by setting it up to look like you'd killed Eubie Kane." He looked at his cell phone. "Third call from the press. Better go and deal with this. Keep me posted, Danny."

The wait for the doctors seemed endless but eventually two of them came into the waiting room. "Is one of you Detective Richardson's partner?" the first one said.

The women looked at each other. "If you mean his professional partner, I am," Danny replied.

"We're authorized to tell you and a woman named Amanda St. Claire what happened to Detective Richardson."

"That's me," Amanda said. "And this is Deputy District

Attorney Margo Keyes."

He looked at the identification Margo pulled out of her purse. "Okay, then, I guess it's all three of you. There's mostly good news. By some miracle, the bullet missed every major organ and artery in Detective Richardson's chest. It nicked his subclavian vein and maybe was diverted by his clavicle. We got the bullet out and I think we got all the bleeders but we'll be keeping a close eye on him to make sure." He looked from one woman to the other. "Any questions?"

"How long will he be in the hospital?" Amanda asked. "And can we see him?"

"We'll put him in ICU overnight to observe him for concussion and then see how he recovers from the surgery. His arm will be in a cast for about six weeks and he'll need physical therapy to make sure he has a full range of motion in his shoulder. You can see him when he gets to ICU. Why don't you wait here and you can go with him when they transfer him."

Knowing that Sam wouldn't want his sons to hear what happened from a television newscast, Amanda called his former wife to alert her. By the time she was off the phone, Danny had left to go back downtown to talk to Drake Vos and begin her reports.

After a few hours, Sam was deemed stable enough to go to ICU and Amanda and Margo accompanied him there. They didn't stay long. Sam had been sedated but the nurse assured Amanda that by the next day he'd be alert and able to talk to her. She suggested Amanda go home and get some sleep.

Yeah, like that was gonna happen.

Chapter Fifteen

Amanda heard the doorbell ring the next morning but didn't bother getting out of bed. It was probably someone going door-to-door selling religion. Or lawn care. The only person she wanted to see at her front door was in the hospital attached to a million machines.

Then Margo Keyes knocked on her bedroom door. "Amanda, are you awake? Danny Hartmann's here. She has a message from Sam."

Amanda was downstairs in seconds. "Sam called you? How is he? What did he say?"

"He called me when he couldn't get you. How come you aren't answering your phones?"

Margo raised her hand. "My fault. Since Amanda didn't have a car at the hospital last night, I drove her home. When I got her here she said she didn't want to be alone, so I stayed. Unplugged her landline phones and turned off her cell. Figured there might be press calling and I didn't want her disturbed."

"How is he?" Amanda asked again.

"He sounded amazingly good. In fact, he was calling with a list of things he wants because he doesn't like what he has in the hospital. I thought maybe you could take them to him, Amanda, as soon as we collect them."

"What's he want?" Amanda asked.

"A pajama top, an electric razor and a cell phone. I picked up a cell phone."

"My brother left an electric razor the last time he was here," Amanda said.

"And, don't ask why, but I have a man's pajama top that should fit Sam," Margo said. "I'll go get it now while you shower and get something to eat, Amanda."

Ninety minutes later, after a hot shower and a breakfast Danny insisted she try to eat, Amanda was at the hospital. She'd had a nervous drive there trying to convince herself Sam would be happy to see her when she wasn't at all sure he would. After all, she was the reason he was in the hospital. He'd been mad about her not telling him what she knew and he didn't know the half of what she'd been keeping from him.

Clutching a plastic bag containing what she'd brought for him, she stopped inside the door of the room and watched him, she wasn't sure for what. Maybe some kind of welcoming sign. But he seemed to be asleep. His eyes were closed, his head half turned away from her. The monitors attached to him were quietly beeping and booping—indicating, apparently, that his heart and whatever else they were monitoring were working correctly because, in spite of the beeps and boops, no one was running to the room with a crash cart.

The edge of the dressing over his surgical incision was visible at the neckline of his hospital gown. His right arm was in a cast. The IV hooked up to his left arm was dripping clear fluids into him, not blood like yesterday. An oxygen cannula was pulled down around his neck. His color was normal and he looked almost rested.

"Hey, baby," Sam interrupted her contemplation of the scene. He opened his eyes, turned toward her and put out his hand. "You gonna just stand there or you gonna come over here? I'd come to you but I'm kinda tied up here."

Stumbling over a chair in her haste to get to his bedside, she dropped the bag as she struggled to regain her balance. When she reached him, she took the hand he held out, blinking back the tears she could feel about to fall. She leaned over, kissed him on the cheek, hoping he wouldn't see how shiny her eyes must be. "How did you know I was here?"

He awkwardly pulled her to him with his casted arm and kissed her on the mouth, held her and kissed her a second time before answering. "It's the way you smell. Like cupcakes, or maybe flowers. Or a flowery cupcake. I don't know. Whatever it is, I could pick you out of a crowd blindfolded." He patted a space on the bed beside him.

She climbed up, not letting go of him when she settled there. "You look so much better. I wasn't sure what to expect."

Using his hand with the IV in it, he clumsily pushed a curl back behind her ear. The familiar gesture made it impossible to contain her tears.

"Please don't cry. I'm fine, now that you're here," he said.

"I'll try." She forced the corners of her mouth up. Clasping his hand to her chest, she asked, "How're you feeling?"

"The truth? Beat up."

"Maybe because you were."

"Yeah, I guess. But I'm doing okay. I'm tougher than a stupid bad guy with a gun." He grinned and kissed her hand. When she pulled it back to her chest, he frowned. "Hey, your heart's beating fast. Maybe you'd like to join me here with a few of these machines attached to you. Not exactly the honeymoon suite but . . . "

She didn't laugh.

"This isn't like that night at the gallery this summer when you were excited to see me. Now you look more scared than happy. How come?"

"I guess I am. More than a little scared, actually." She dropped her eyes for a moment and her voice became softer. "I wasn't sure you'd want to see me." A lump materialized in her throat. She gulped it down so she could talk. "This is my fault. All of it. I'm the reason you got shot and ended up here. I'm so, so sorry, Sam. I messed up so bad."

"You messed up? How's this your fault?" he asked.

"I thought if I gave him the money he wanted, he'd leave you alone. If I'd done better at it or if I'd trusted you and Danny with what I knew . . . "

"What? You gave who what?"

"I let Matthews think I knew about the safe, about Tommy's money. I didn't think there was a safe but I had money so I . . . "

"What the hell did you do something like that for? Christ, Amanda, he could have hurt you. He could have killed you." The warm affectionate expression she'd been greeted with was now the set-in-stone angry look she'd seen too often recently.

"After last year, I couldn't let you get hurt, couldn't let you get involved. I just did what I thought would keep him away from you until Danny, Detective Hartmann . . . "

"I know who Danny is. What I don't know is why the hell you did something this reckless."

The tears were streaking down her cheeks now and she thought she could hear the sound of his heart rate increasing on one of the machines. "I'm sorry. I was stupid. I didn't tell you or Danny what I knew. All I could think of was protecting you. I . . . I love you. I couldn't let you . . . "

"Wait, say that again."

"What?"

"The part about loving me."

She tried smiling but her mouth wobbled. "I love you, Sam."

"That's a hell of a way to get me to stop being pissed off at you."

"Did it work?" The smile came a little easier this time.

"Come here and find out." He reached for her and she slipped her arms around his neck and moved in for a kiss. He tried to circle her with his arms but the cast, the IV and the cords and cables got in the way and they gave up.

When she sat up, he said, "Amanda, you shouldn't have tried to deal with him on your own. And you better never do anything even remotely like that again. But you didn't put me here. Matthews did. He and Vos and Tom Webster are responsible. Hell, add me to the list. I shouldn't have let my pride make me angry; I should have seen how scared you were. I should have . . . well, I didn't.

But it's over now. The Webster case is finally all over." He brought her fingers to his mouth and kissed them.

She held his hand to her chest again. "On the way here this morning, I wondered. Maybe you wouldn't want to see me, maybe you'd discovered something . . . "

His laugh interrupted. "I've discovered I don't like being shot and I don't like being in the hospital. Does that count?"

"I'm serious, Sam."

"So am I, believe me." He laced his finger through hers. "What do you think I might change my mind about, pretty lady?"

"I don't know. Maybe you'd want to make changes in your life." She paused and tilted her head down to hide the expression on her face. "Maybe be with someone else. Someone who doesn't make you angry by doing stupid things."

He turned her face up so she was looking at him. "I was angry because I was frustrated, worried about you being safe. I don't want to be with someone else. Why would I?"

She grabbed tissues from the box on his bedside stand and dabbed at her eyes. "We haven't exactly been Romeo and Juliet lately."

"Christ, I hope not. Look how they ended up."

"I meant . . . "

"Forget Romeo and Juliet. How about us, the way things were before you tried to protect me. I don't need you to protect me from a bad guy, but I do need you. I love you."

After another attempt at kissing resulted in the same tangle of cords and IV lines, they settled for talking. As they spoke, she touched the bruises on his face, the dressing on his incision, the cast on his arm as if her touch would hasten the healing.

The ICU staff left them alone even though she was clearly exceeding the time limits for visitors. Eventually they were interrupted by the surgeons on rounds who released Sam to the surgical floor and from most of the machines that had been monitoring him. Amanda packed up the few pieces of clothing they hadn't cut off him the day before and carried them downstairs to a room he had all to himself.

After making sure Sam was comfortable in his new bed, Amanda said, "I think it's time for me to go. I've already overstayed my time. But I'll be back tonight."

"Don't go. There's nothing to do here except annoy the nurses if you're not here," he threatened.

"When I come back I'll bring you a couple books and my iPod with music you'll like. You need to rest. You're recuperating from life-threatening injuries."

"I'm fine."

"That's why they had all that gear attached to you? " she said.

"They're overcautious. I'm fine."

"I don't know about fine but you are incorrigible." She bent down and kissed him. "Behave yourself. Sleep. Don't torture the staff."

Amanda left the hospital feeling a great weight had been lifted from her. She was so overjoyed she realized when she put the key in the ignition that she couldn't remember taking the elevator to the lobby, finding her SUV or getting into it. She sat for a few moments with her head on the steering wheel, giving thanks to whatever power watched over police officers.

"Amanda? Are you okay?" Danny Hartmann said as she knocked gently on the driver's side window.

Amanda sat up slowly. "I'm fine. I'm tired. But everything's okay."

"Sam's doing better?"

"He's been moved out of ICU; he's got most of the machines off; he's complaining about being in the hospital. Yeah, I'd say he's doing better."

"Ah, the real Sam has returned. Care to bet on how long it'll take the nurses to figure out they liked him better unconscious?"

"I don't think you can bet on things that have already happened. We're going to have to bribe them not to gag and restrain him before this is all over."

Chapter Sixteen

Sam amazed his doctors with his rapid recovery. He attributed it to his fitness and good health. They thought it might have something to do with the constant attention he got from the women in his life. His partner dropped in when she could. Amanda was there all day, every day, of his short stay. And his sister came over from Eastern Oregon to see for herself that he was okay, providing stories about her baby brother's childhood escapades that embarrassed him and delighted Amanda.

The other women who interacted with him on a regular basis, however, weren't so impressed with Sam. Restless to be out from under every restriction the nurses tried to impose, he was not an easy patient. As she'd predicted she would have to do, Amanda brought bribes to the staff at every visit—candy, fruit, small glass ornaments, large containers of gourmet coffee—anything to try and mitigate for Sam's grumpy resistance to the rules they attempted to enforce. When Amanda reminded him he once said he liked rules, he replied he only liked them when he was doing the enforcing.

The struggle between Sam and the medical staff came to a head the day the doctors told him he couldn't be released from the hospital until he arranged assistance in his apartment for at least two to three weeks. No matter how much he argued, they wouldn't budge. He was there until he made satisfactory plans for his home care. Or they'd do it for him.

When Amanda arrived that afternoon, her favorite nurse explained what the doctors had told him and warned her that Sam wasn't happy about it. In fact, she suggested Amanda might want to go home and come back after he'd cooled down.

Amanda found him pacing the hall outside his room. "Hey, cowboy, rumor has it you've had a bad day."

"Goddamn doctors. Why the hell do they think they know better than I do what I can or can't do? I don't need Nurse Ratched or some strange man—they said they would arrange a male nurse if I wanted one. Christ, that's all I need."

"If you'll stop ranting and stand still, I'll kiss you hello."

"Sorry, baby." He held her and she kissed him. "I can't stand being here for another couple days until they make arrangements."

"Not happy appears to be an understatement. But I've got an idea that might make you feel better. Let's go back in your room and talk."

They walked toward his room, his casted arm around her shoulders. "What, you have the name of someone who can come in and help me?"

"Not exactly." She led him to the two chairs next to the window. "Suppose you had a place to go where there'd be help available twenty-four seven? Would that satisfy the doctors?"

"Some kind of nursing home? They said that, too. Absolutely not."

"No, I'm thinking my house." Ignoring the startled look on his face, she continued. "If you recuperated with me, I'd be able to help you. I could change your dressing and take you to your appointments. I can cook, help you with meals."

The startled look was slowly being replaced with the wisp of a smile playing around his lips. "How about showering? Would you help me shower?"

"If you need help, of course."

"Oh, I'm sure I'd need help." The smile had taken control of his mouth and was moving up through his dimple to the crinkles around his eyes. "And where would I sleep?"

"Wherever you'd like. I have four bedrooms. Take your pick."

"Suppose I pick yours? Would you be there, too?"

"That could be arranged, assuming it doesn't interfere with your rest."

"You sleeping beside me would never interfere with me. Of course, I can't promise I won't try to interfere with you." A full-fledged grin appeared on his face. "This shitty day has suddenly gotten a helluva lot better."

"I'm glad you like my idea."

The grin faded as fast as it had appeared. He cocked his head, frowning. "Seriously, are you sure? You're not doing this because you think you owe me something or you're feeling guilty or responsible for what happened or bullshit like that, are you?" he asked. "I don't need you to feel sorry for me."

"I'm doing this because I want to. Because I thought it would solve your problem, and make you happy. Because . . . " she paused.

"Because?" he prompted.

"Because this will probably be the only chance I'll ever have to take care of you. Or, maybe more accurately, the only time you'll ever let me take care of you. So, let me."

The smile was back although a bit wary. "Okay, your house it is. But, just so you know, once I move in, you may have a helluva time getting me out."

"We'll worry about that later, if we have to." She attempted to stand up but he held on to her. "If you'll let me go, I'll have the nurses page your doctor and see if this works for him. If he'll agree to let you go tomorrow, I'll take your keys and move things from your apartment to my house so it's all ready for you."

"I'll move stuff to your house when I get out of here."

"No, you won't. There is a condition attached to this offer—you have to do exactly what the doctors tell you to do. If you don't, I swear I'll hire an eighty-year-old nurse in a bikini to shower you and take a photo of it for Danny to show around the precinct."

"Christ, she'd love that. Okay, I'll find out what the rules are."

"*I'll* find out what the rules are."

"You don't trust me?" His grin was sly now.

"I trust you about everything. Anything. Anything, that is, except an accurate recital of the restrictions the doctors will put on you. That I don't trust you about."

"You're probably right." He let go of her hand. "Okay, call the doc and see what he says. If he says no, tell him I can always sign myself out. See what he comes back with after that."

"This isn't a hostage negotiation, Sam."

"Sure as hell feels like one to me."

The surgeon agreed to her plan. After asking if she knew what she was getting into, he gave her a five-minute crash course in how to take care of a curmudgeonly patient with a cast on his arm and a fresh surgical incision, and said he'd leave discharge prescriptions at the nurses' station in the morning when he made rounds.

He answered all her questions about Sam's restrictions, which included no weight on his arms, no lifting anything heavy with his uncasted arm because of the incision, no driving, horseback riding, running or weight lifting. Wondering how willing and cooperative Sam would be when she got him home, Amanda went back down the hall to break the good news.

Chapter Seventeen

Getting his stuff from his apartment was easy. Getting him out of the hospital the next day was more complicated. Amanda brought his favorite cowboy boots and a pair of jeans, along with a blue, button-down shirt, thinking only of what he'd be most comfortable in, not of the logistics of getting him into the clothes with a cast and an impaired shoulder.

When she asked if he wanted help he turned her down. After he struggled a bit, he admitted she was going to have to assist. As she helped him with his shirt, he grumbled that he like it better when she undressed him. Amanda could barely keep a straight face.

Next came the inevitable fight over riding to the car in a wheelchair. "Hospital policy," the nurse said. "Fuck hospital policy," Sam responded. But she made it clear he couldn't get signed out until he sat in it. Amanda left in the middle of the standoff, sure the nurse would win, and went to get her SUV.

Sam rode downstairs in the wheelchair but claimed a small moral victory by jumping out of it just before they got to the front door. Before the nurse turned to go back with the empty chair Amanda thought she saw an expression of relief that would seem to indicate she was happy Sam was now someone else's problem.

Their arrival at Amanda's place was easier. He hopped out of the Highlander as soon as she turned off the ignition and almost ran to the door. Chihuly greeted them with enthusiasm. Sam knelt and there was face licking (by Chihuly) and ear scratching (by Sam) while Amanda emptied the car of the books, flowers, and personal items from the hospital.

"Want to go upstairs and see where I put your things?" she asked when she'd brought in the last load.

"Might as well, sure."

She showed him where she'd put his clothes and began to explain where things were in the bathroom. Then she caught his reflection in the mirror. He was running his hand over his face, not seeming to register what she was saying. "You can change anything around that you want, Sam. I . . . "

"No, it's fine. Whatever you did is fine."

"What's going on?" she asked, still looking at him in the mirror.

"Nothing. I'm fine."

She turned around. "If you're having second thoughts about the arrangement, if you'd rather be at your apartment, I understand. We can unravel all this, make other arrangements. But if we're going to change things, we should do it before it gets more complicated."

He took the few steps he needed to get close enough to put his arms around her. "I'm not having second thoughts. I want to be here. It's just . . . "

"It's just . . . what?" She touched his face and ran her thumb across the bruise on his cheek. "Tell me, please."

"I wanted to get out of the damn hospital so bad I didn't think about what it would be like when I was released. Maybe expecting things to go back to the way they were before is too much to ask right now."

"What things?"

"Like . . . " He paused and scanned her face. "Oh, hell, it's me. I feel . . . detached, maybe. Nothing seems normal." He blew out a breath. "I just need a couple good nights' sleep. I didn't get much in the hospital."

"Do you want to reconsider where you're sleeping? Maybe one of the guest rooms would be better after all."

He rubbed his hand over his face again.

"Was it noisy staff or bad dreams in the hospital?" she asked when he didn't respond.

"Both."

She took his hand and played with his fingers, then traced the veins on the back of his hand, not looking at him. "Have I ever told you why I got Chihuly?"

"Wasn't it for security?"

"Not really. I got him because I was having such a hard time in Seattle that I wondered if I'd made a mistake accepting the residency at Pilchuck. I'd begun to have horrible dreams, nightmares really, after Tommy died and they didn't stop after I moved. Cynthia suggested I get a pet and told me about this breeder who had a new litter of curly coated retrievers."

"All with names of people with curly black hair."

"Exactly. At first, I let Chihuly sleep with me, to get him used to being without his littermates, I told myself. In truth, I loved having a warm furry ball of puppy next to me in bed. And when I'd wake up crying from a nightmare, he'd lick my face. It was probably because he liked the salt in my tears but it was comforting. A week or so after I got him, the dreams stopped."

She looked up just as he smiled.

"So, you'll lick my face when I have a bad dream?" he asked.

"That's not where I was going with this, Sam. I just meant it takes some time to feel normal again, to get past something bad. But you will."

In response, he kissed her, a tender, sweet kiss, full of hope and affection.

She broke from his embrace just as he was turning it into something more serious and said, "How about I fix lunch for us? And then maybe you'd like a shower?"

"Umm, a shower. I would have killed for a shower in the hospital." He took her hand and kissed it. "Does helping me shower involve you naked?"

"I got a hand-held shower head so you can keep the water off your cast and . . . "

"You're not answering the question, Amanda."

Without replying, she headed for the hall. "Come on, I roasted a chicken for sandwiches and made potato salad. And there are fresh tomatoes and pears and grapes."

Hesitating for a moment, he finally followed, Chihuly trailing after him. "Is this like the first time I stayed over? You had enough breakfast in the refrigerator to feed the precinct."

"If you're not in the mood for chicken and potato salad, there's ham and cheese. I can make tuna salad. Of course, I can do grilled cheese. Oh, and I have a panini machine so I could make anything into one of those. There's falafel and hummus on pita bread, if you want to go vegetarian. There's also macaroni salad—it's from New Seasons, I didn't make it—and I have lettuce so we can put together a green salad . . . "

"Are you planning anything other than stuffing me with food while I recuperate?"

*

After lunch, Amanda took Chihuly for a walk. Left to himself, Sam went into the living room armed with a new thriller by his favorite writer to divert his attention from . . . well, from a lot of things, now that he thought about it. But after he'd read the first chapter twice trying to get into the story, he put the book down, wondering if the writer had lost his edge. He tried a second book and when that didn't make any more sense than the first one had, he decided the writers were just fine. He was the problem. Pacing up and down didn't distract him either, so he put in a CD, and lay back on the couch.

But his mind wouldn't shut off. He'd been only half-truthful when he'd told Amanda what was bothering him. Yes, he was feeling a bit off-balance after being shot and in the hospital, but he was even more uneasy about being at Amanda's house. In spite of what she'd said, he wondered if she'd only volunteered to help him while he recuperated because she felt guilty about what happened. He didn't want her to pity him, to take care of him like he was some kind of damned charity case. He wanted Amanda to love him.

She'd said the words, once. But that was when he was in the hospital and she thought she'd put him there. And, okay, she'd pecked him on the cheek every time she came to see him, but she hadn't held him or really kissed him since they'd had their last dinner together, whenever the hell that was. And upstairs today she'd backed away just when the kiss was getting interesting. Not to mention suggesting he sleep someplace other than with her. What the hell was that about?

Suppose she expected him to leave when he was cleared to go back to his job? What would he do then? He hadn't been kidding when he said he wouldn't want to move out once he moved in. If he'd had his way, he would have given notice to his landlord before he left the hospital.

He heard the sound of the door unlocking, the clunk of her keys as she tossed them onto the table in the hall, the thud of her shoes as she took them off and tossed them under the table. Chihuly came bounding in, eager for a drink and a little rest, Amanda with him, presumably on her way to the kitchen to clean up the lunch dishes.

Might as well get it over with. At least he'd know where he stood.

He beckoned to her. "Hey, come here, pretty lady." He rose from the couch, as she got closer.

"Do you need something?"

"Yeah, I need you." He held out his hand. "I put on your favorite Tom Grant CD."

"I hear." She ignored his outstretched hand.

The sounds of *Gold* began and he put his arms around her

waist. "This sounds like a song you can dance to."

"I thought you said . . ."

" . . . I wasn't good at dancing?" He pulled her closer. "I'm not. Except for the slow ones."

"Rubbing up against each other while music plays isn't dancing, Sam." She rested her hand on his good shoulder.

"It's fun, though, don't you think?"

She looked sternly at him. "Shouldn't you be resting instead of dancing? You're supposed to be recuperating, and the doctor said that meant mostly resting. You promised. I still have the address of that eighty-year-old nurse and she still has a bikini."

"I was resting on the couch. Couldn't get more rest-ier than that." He nestled her head on his chest. He didn't want to look at her when he asked what he needed to ask. "I thought I'd check with you one more time . . . are you really okay with this?"

"What 'this' do you mean? The 'this' that you can't dance or the 'this' of your being here?"

"That one."

She pulled back and cocked her head, a puzzled expression on her face that slowly changed to amusement. "Oh, my God, you're still worried about why I offered to have you move in, aren't you? I thought you were more secure than that. What happened to my tough cop who couldn't be brought down by a stupid bad guy?"

"I'm not so tough when it comes to you, baby."

Smiling at him, she put her hands on either side of his face. "I'm not sure whether I'm more flattered or amused that you're still concerned. But for the record, I want you here because I love you. I've loved you for longer than I was willing to admit, even to myself. Then, about the time I finally faced it, it seemed like last year was happening all over again and telling you got lost in trying to keep everything from falling apart again." Gently she kissed him, nibbling on his lower lip when she ended it, as if reluctant to let go of him.

"But having you here, I have another chance. So, it's too bad about the not dancing thing but we can work on that. While you're here. Because I'm really happy about that. And if it turns out you never go back to your apartment, I'll be really happy about that, too. Is that the answer you were angling for?"

He answered without words, capturing her mouth with his. Her lips parted so he could taste her with his tongue. Her back arched, her hips pushed against him. His erection pressed into her as he slid his hands down her back and molded her against him.

"Any more questions, cowboy?" she whispered as she kissed down his jaw line to his neck.

"Just one more." His hand went under her sweater and cupped a breast. He rolled her nipple between his fingers and felt it harden at his touch. "It's been a while so tell me if I'm wrong, but don't I start here?"

"Please, Sam. Be careful."

His hand froze in place. "Did something happen to your breast?"

"Not my breast. Your incision."

"My incision's fine. The doctor said if I was careful, I could begin to do normal things."

"And you thought immediately of sex."

"Well, that's normal, isn't it? And I asked him about it. I have to keep my weight off my arms but that's okay." He grinned at her. "You can do most of the work. All I have to do is relax and enjoy myself."

"I asked him, too." He didn't try to hide his surprise—his delight—that she'd asked. "I knew you'd ask and I wanted to make sure we heard the same answer."

"Did we?"

"Yes, but . . . "

"So, while I'm on vacation we can make up for lost time. I thought we'd start now."

Now she was startled. "Vacation? Recuperating from a gunshot wound is a vacation?"

"Well, I'm not working so it must be a vacation."

"And your idea of how to spend your time on this vacation-slash-recuperation is, what, sex and a little light reading?"

He pushed up the rest of her sweater with his good hand and began to massage the other breast. "Yup. Maybe just sex without the reading." He pulled at the button on her jeans and managed with one hand to get the zipper down. "Have I ever told you that I love it that you don't wear a bra?"

She smiled. "Yes, usually when we're half-undressed and headed for bed."

He kissed her neck and ran his hand up her bare back.

"Sam, what am I going to do with you?"

"I thought that was obvious. But if you want me to be specific, I thought we'd . . . "

She drew his mouth to hers, her lips parting, making a foray with the tip of her tongue, teasing, tasting, as the kiss deepened.

Without breaking contact with any part of her, he moved back toward the couch.

"What're you doing? I thought we were going to bed," she whispered against his lips.

"Here's closer."

Two pairs of jeans hit the floor. He was about to lower himself onto the couch when he stopped. "Oh, hell. We have to go upstairs. I don't have any protection."

"Look in your back jeans pocket."

He picked up the jeans and found the condom tucked there. "How'd that get there?"

"I put it there. It was sort of a welcome home thing. But you didn't notice it. Guess I should have been more obvious about where I put it."

"Wish I'd found it earlier. I wouldn't have worried so much

about that suggestion I sleep in another room." He shed his boxer briefs, then stooped to inch her scrap-of-lace thong off her. She helped by trying to wiggle out of it, making her breasts bounce close to his mouth, which went dry at the thought of suckling them.

But she took over before he could act on the thought. Gently pushing him down onto the leather couch, she straddled his body. With painstaking care, she opened his shirt so she could touch his bare skin, stroke his chest, massage his undamaged shoulder.

Then, after rolling the condom over his erection, she planted her fists on either side of his head and moved her body against him, grazing his chest with her breasts and rubbing the cleft of her sex against his penis.

He groaned. "God, woman, you're killing me."

"I've missed you. I've missed this." With little love bites, she nipped at his mouth, his jaw, his neck.

"Please, just let me . . . " He touched her, felt how ready she was for him. Stroking her, inserting his fingers into the wet center of her, he tried to position his hips so he could enter her but she wouldn't let him.

"Not yet. Just kissing now." This time, however, when she moved to kiss him, he guided himself into her. She gasped, pushed his good arm back over his head. "I thought I was in charge here," she said.

"Okay, baby, you be in charge. What do you want?" he asked in a hoarse whisper.

"This. Just this." She began to move her hips slowly and deliberately. He let her set the rhythm at first. Sipping and licking her way from his mouth to his neck and back up again, she eluded his attempts to change the pace, to hold her close, pushing away his arm when he tried to pin her, to keep her close to him. When he swore under his breath in frustration, she just laughed.

Finally, he ended her game by corralling her with his casted arm and holding her to him. His mouth took possession of hers; his tongue played sexy games. With his cock deep inside her, thrusting harder and faster, she came in a shuddering climax and so did he.

When they returned to earth, he snuggled her against him, kissing her damp forehead.

"I've never made love in the living room before," she said, when her breathing calmed.

"Sex on the nearest horizontal surface with half your clothes on isn't what I'd call making love," he said as he gave her breasts one last caress and pulled down her sweater, which had bunched up around her neck.

She returned the favor, readjusting his shirt. "And what would you call it, cowboy?"

"I think you know."

"You want to hear me say the word, don't you?"

"I don't think I've ever heard you say it, have I?"

"Probably not." She waited for him to change his mind but he was apparently not going to back off. "Okay, it's fucking. Sex on the couch with us half dressed is fucking. Happy?"

He kissed her cheek, his grin so broad he thought his face would crack. "Yeah, I'm happy but not because of that. I'm happy because I love you, because we're . . . "

"Hey, stop that." She was laughing.

"Stop what? Telling you I love you? Don't you like hearing it?"

"No . . . I mean, yes, I like hearing it. I didn't mean *you* should stop. I meant Chihuly should stop. He's licking my toes and it tickles. What do you call sex on the couch with a dog licking your foot?"

"Our idea of normal, baby. It's our idea of normal."

Acknowledgments

As anyone who appreciates studio art glass knows, the Bullseye Resource Center and factory is a very real place. For over a decade, I've benefited from living a half-hour away from the place where some of the most beautiful glass ever created for an artist to use is manufactured. I can't say "thank you" enough to the staff, teachers and talented artists there who've always answered my questions, fed my passion and helped me grow as an artisan and as a teacher.

Which means I have to apologize for two things: first, for turning your workplace into a crime scene in my story. And I'm sorry I couldn't respond to the request for a staff vote on who the murder victim would be. I was afraid it might be me.

However, as real as Bullseye is, all the events and people portrayed in this novel are fictional. Only the fabulous glass is true to life.

About the Author

Peggy Bird lives with her husband in Vancouver, Washington where she writes and does kiln-formed glass across the Columbia River from Portland, Oregon where her three daughters, assorted grandchildren and grand-dogs, and Bullseye Glass live.

If you liked Sam and Amanda's story, you might enjoy Liz and Collins' story, *Beginning Again* available now from Crimson Romance. In 2013, Crimson Romance will release *Closing Arguments,* the story of Margo and Tony.

In the mood for more Crimson Romance? Check out *Night Blooming Jasmine* by Alicia Thorne at *CrimsonRomance.com*.

21176079R00090

Made in the USA
Lexington, KY
02 March 2013